NOAH
Voyage To A New Earth

D1022467

Christian Jr./Sr. High School
2100 Greenfield Dr
El Cajon, CA 92019

NOAH
Voyage To A New Earth

T 15224

J. R. LUCAS

Christian Jr./Sr High School
2100 Greenfield Dr
El Cajon, CA 92019

Wolgemuth & Hyatt, Publishers, Inc.
Brentwood, Tennessee

The mission of Wolgemuth & Hyatt, Publishers, Inc. is to publish and distribute books that lead individuals toward:

- A personal faith in the one true God: Father, Son, and Holy Spirit;

- A lifestyle of practical discipleship; and

- A worldview that is consistent with the historic, Christian faith.

Moreover, the Company endeavors to accomplish this mission at a reasonable profit and in a manner which glorifies God and serves His Kingdom.

© 1991 by J. R. Lucas. All rights reserved.
Published March 1991. First Edition.
Printed in the United States of America.
97 96 95 94 93 92 91   8 7 6 5 4 3 2 1

No part of this publication may be reproduced, stored in a retrieval system, or transmitted in any form by any means, electronic, mechanical, photocopy, recording, or otherwise, without the prior written permission of the publisher, except for brief quotations in critical reviews or articles.

Wolgemuth & Hyatt, Publishers, Inc.
1749 Mallory Lane, Suite 110
Brentwood, Tennessee 37027

Library of Congress Cataloging-in-Publication Data

Lucas, J. R. (James Raymond), 1950–
    Noah : Voyage to a New Earth / J. R. Lucas. — 1st ed.
        p.   cm.
    ISBN 1-56121-053-6
    1. Noah (Biblical figure) — Fiction. 2. Bible. O.T. — History of
Biblical events — Fiction. I. Title.
PS3562.U235N64 1991
813'.54 — dc20   90-28852
                                                            CIP

For All of My Loved Ones, of Course

ACKNOWLEDGMENTS

M y wife, Pamela, for continual inspiration, support, careful editing, and joyful labor; my daughter, Laura Christine, for encouragement and helpful comments; my son, Peter Barrett, for love and encouragement; my spiritual daughter, Maryl Jan, for reading, thoughtful input, and encouragement; Tom Willis (president) and Dave Foran of Creation Science Association for Mid-America for their helpful suggestions; and Mike Hyatt and the excellent staff at Wolgemuth & Hyatt, for their vision for this book, hard work, and the pleasure of partnership.

CHAPTER 1

T he man stood with his hands on his hips and stared at the view-imager in front of him. Frustration filled his usually joyous face. He shook his head as he thought how the project was progressing compared with the timeplan. He was at least two months behind—not against a meaningless date, but against an immovable point in time, a point beyond which lay only failure and death.

He thought back to ten years before, when he had first gotten the clear vision for the project. In their search for success, most people even then had turned to the world of commerce, to the pursuit of money to satisfy their desire to be free from authority. Others who desired power had turned to the realm of government.

Few, it seemed to him, had had a higher vision for their lives then, or even long before that in the days of his youth. But even in his loftiest imaginations, he had never expected to be involved with such an incredible project.

The project. It had started with a flurry as he felt the urgency to complete it as soon as possible. As time passed, and as he began to realize how difficult the effort was going to be, the magnitude of what he had begun overwhelmed him. His enthusiasm lagged at times; the project was just so huge and the time so short. The project was consuming so much of his time and resources that even his children had questioned him on the clarity of his vision on many occasions.

But the thought that the project might not be finished in time drove him back to his view-imager and to the project itself. He had only one certainty to which he could cling: the absolute confidence that there was a rightness about this creative work, a rightness that would someday bring him total vindication.

But tonight he was tired. As he had stretched his days into the early morning hours, his fatigue had grown. He had been trying to get by on four hours of sleep a night, and it just wasn't enough. His wife had tried to persuade him to get more sleep, but he had resisted. Time was too precious.

He touched several presspoints that straightened the image. He touched another presspoint, and bright colored light poured from the shining glass. He could see the structural components, as drawn and intensified by the logicbox, in vivid red. Other facets of the project were displayed in a wide variety of extremely intense colors.

He touched the presspoint marked "eliminate," and then entered the command "all except type seven." Immediately everything was eliminated from the view-imager except for the structural components. Then he quickly touched the presspoint marked "close in," and with the help of the power-writer began to outline the bottom fourth of the project.

When he completed the drawing, the outlined section expanded to fill the shining glass. He then touched the presspoint marked "rotate," and the image began to turn. He smiled faintly as it began its second circuit. This part was good, he thought; the designer had earned his pay with his work on this part of the imaging. This section should withstand all of the forces that might be applied to it.

He was almost too tired to stand. He put the power-writer in its retainer and moved slowly to his bodyrest. As he leaned back, he could hear the central music machine playing softly. The music took hold of him in a special way that only music tied to pleasant memories could do.

It was his favorite song ever played by anyone on the cadicord. He'd first heard it when he'd received one of the first memorypacks covering the events of the Third Revolution. Less than an hour into the viewing of those events, he had become bored with the sameness in the storyteller's voice and offended by the inaccurate recounting of an event that he himself still had clearly in his mind. He smiled as he thought of the irony of calling this a "memorypack" when it was totally false.

But just as he had decided to end the viewing, the scene had shifted to a greenspace where the trees had been planted in coils to reflect the design of the human bodycode. It was a beautiful view, one that had immediately settled him back into his bodyrest.

And then the music started, a lilting, lifting work that moved him quickly to tears. The aroma of grass and flowers came out of the memorypack and filled the room. The music, the greenspace, the smell of the flowers in the air, filling every breath, all combined to give him an unforgettable memory.

This same music had given him such encouragement when his third child was born. His wife had gone into labor early, and although the doctors had many things to offer, he knew in his heart that his wife and child were in the hands of God. Although the doctors had been using artificial wombs to save babies as early as fifteen weeks after conception, he knew that his wife—only twelve weeks along—was really beyond the ability of the doctors to help.

So he and his wife had prayed. They had spent hours together, talking and praying. His great-grandfather's lifecord had been a tremendous source of encouragement during that time. They were amazed, as they viewed the lifecord and as they thought of the depravity of their own time, that such a man could have actually existed. But his lifecord was clear, and listening to his own words gave them the confidence to trust in their God.

And then there was the music. Whenever his wife's labor would begin, he would put the beautiful song into the central machine, and he and his wife would sit close together and listen. It was almost like listening to the voice of God, and it always reminded them of Him.

And their child had been born safely, twenty-two weeks after conception.

The doctors had pushed him to let them do a bodycode search, to see if the child would be healthy and capable. Although the civil government's Mastermen supported forced searches, such searches were not absolute law. Nevertheless, the doctors were still persuasive in convincing a vast number of people to choose to submit to the searches. Many mothers, who had the sole right to choose light disintegration for their unborn children (or "nonpersons," as the doctors always called them), then took this step, often believing that their decisions had been made for the benefit of the child within.

But he and his wife had refused to submit to the searches. And other than having one lung removed and sent to the region's healing center for rebuilding and coating, the child had no other difficulties. The little sickly child was now tall and strong and about to be married.

When the music was over, the man looked through the large window at the end of the room. He saw the sun as it stood just above the horizon and watched several streams of light pour over the lower valley. He couldn't believe that in the midst of such beauty, men and women could be so ugly, so wicked, so depraved.

But they were. Just two months before he had been walking through the crystal part of the city and had seen a man beating a child unmercifully. The child—a girl—was cursing the man with foul language. The hatred between the man and the girl was beyond comprehension. He had quickly found a commander and asked him to stop the beating. The commander had gone to the attacker, who had abruptly stopped beating the girl and had shown the commander something. Incredibly, the commander had walked away and the man had begun to beat the child again.

The commander had come back to him. "Nothing I can do," he had said, indifferently.

"What do you mean?" he had asked in a choking voice.

"She's a kind five," the commander had said bluntly. "Don't get many of them around here, which is why it seems so unusual. As I'm sure you know, kind fives don't get any protection by the government."

He had started to go toward the attacker, but the commander had stopped him. "Let me go," he had screamed at the commander. "She's just a little girl!"

"She *isn't* just a little girl," the commander had said without emotion. "She's a kind five. She's of no importance to anyone. She's useless." The commander had grabbed his arms, quickly pulled them behind his back, and slipped retainers on them.

"She's better off dead," the commander had concluded. Efforts to break free had been painful and ineffective. Every time he moved, the commander hit him in the side. As the commander began to drag him away, he heard a final scream which told him that the child was dead. After the attacker had gone away, the commander had removed the re-

tainers. After the commander had called for a "pickup" of the body, he
had walked off, shaking his head.

He had kneeled next to the little girl's body and cried for a long
time. After the regional transport took the body away, he had gone to
see his grandfather again. His grandfather was a very old man.

"I agree things are bad, but it's been a long time since you could
really say that God took any direct action against evil," his grandfather
had said. "Things have been quiet for a long time."

"Not so quiet, grandfather," he had disagreed softly. "He *is* talking;
it's just that no one is listening."

His sister, who had entered the room as he finished speaking,
scolded him. "I know you think you have some great vision for what's
going to happen in the future, and you think that fool project of yours is
going to make a difference, but you're so wrong I can hardly make
myself talk to you." She had glared at him. "You're right when you say
that things are bad and that people are doing things they shouldn't be
doing, but you're wrong when you say that God is going to . . . kill
them all."

She had taken a seat next to her grandfather. "God doesn't judge
anymore; He works on the idea of grace. He gives us unconditional
love, no matter what we do. Besides, isn't death enough of a punishment?" She had looked at the old man sitting next to her, and then back
at him. "I'd like to be proud of you, but I think I have to agree with my
son—you're a fool for wasting your time on that project. I don't know
why our father supported you until his death."

The words still stung him. And his grandfather, full of uncertainty,
had not come to his defense.

He had come back from his grandfather's with new determination to
finish the project on or ahead of the timeplan. He had run and rerun the
logicbox hundreds of times, getting variations on the number of workers
required and when and where they should be brought in to help. He had
pushed himself so hard for the last two months that he couldn't even
remember what day of the week it was.

                              ❧ ❧ ❧

"Hello, friend," said his wife, who was standing at the door.

"Hello, Tess," he said, forcing a smile. "How has your day been?"

"Busy. The real question is, 'how has it been up here?'"

"Some of the images had serious problems," he said flatly. "Most people just don't care about their work anymore. Not believing in the project doesn't help either."

"It doesn't matter that they don't believe in your project," she answered confidently. "It only matters that *you* believe in God, and that *He* believes in your project."

He smiled, stood up, and walked over to her. Holding her face in his hands, he looked into her eyes. Her round face was etched with beautiful, flowing lines, and her green eyes shone like emeralds. Her light brown hair draped over his hands, framing her face. As he gazed into her eyes, he delighted in seeing her love pour through her broad smile.

"Tess," he said gently, "you always know what to say. You've been with me on this from the beginning. God sure knew what kind of wife I needed — one who not only would love me, but who would actually try to keep me convinced that I'm not out of my mind!"

They both laughed.

"Are you going to be at it all night?" she asked softly, as she put her hands on his arms and studied his face. She delighted in his eyes, dark brown and now so tired, which could speak either firmness or tenderness so well.

"No, I don't think so," he said. "I've actually been thinking about a lot of other things, including that little girl who was beaten to death."

"That was terrible!" she said angrily. "I don't know how much worse the violence can get before God really does do what you've been saying for years." She looked up at him. "Oh, no, you don't!" she said in a gently scolding manner. "You don't need to think about these things, and you know that if I do I spend all my time worrying about them. I think you need to do something else."

"You're probably right," he agreed, letting her go and sitting down. "In fact, I was just thinking about my great-grandfather's lifecord, and how encouraging it always is. Tess, I think I might go watch it for a while."

She brightened up. "I think that's a great idea. I'll go get you a drink and something to eat, and you can get into the big bodyrest in the viewing room."

He kissed her and went into the next room while she went to the downstairs area. He turned on the viewlife and entered the memorypack marked "Lifecords 20." The titles of each of the lifecords stored on the memorypack began to move across the viewlife slowly. He scanned for several minutes until he found the one he wanted. He touched a presspoint and was notified that the lifecord would begin in one minute.

As he sat down in the bodyrest, the friendly face that he had never known in life came on. He sat back, amazed that he could actually watch and listen to a man who had been dead for so many years. The restorers had done excellent work with the old material. The lifecord still looked old, but the image was clear.

"Hello, my child," the rich voice began. "My name is Enoch, of the seventh generation from Adam." The friendly face smiled at him, and he smiled back. "The year of this lifecord is 986 A.C. I have much to tell you about what I have learned in my 364 years."

Tess brought him food and drink, kissed him, and then excused herself to get some sleep.

And Noah watched the lifecord well into the night.

CHAPTER 2

The dawn, as always, was beautiful. The shimmering red sun seemed very distant as it broke through the unchanging cloud canopy. The air was soft and warm. The distant mountains to the south painted a dark line across the horizon.

Noah stood on the hill to the west of the project, looking back and forth between the sunrise and the mountains. He let his gaze drift slowly to the north, where in the distance the huge city of his birth began to take shape through the early morning haze.

Noah looked down at the project. Already the sounds of men and tools filled the air—the sound of a powercutter on the far side of the ship and the sharp cracking of a hammer coming from somewhere on the northern side, just inside the great door. He watched several men on platforms working on the substructure near the end closest to him. The sharp smell of the forming equipment came from the area where the workers were fabricating the skeleton of the great ship. He smiled as he thought of Japheth's word for the oddly designed ship. From the beginning he had called it "the box."

"So many men," Noah muttered to himself, "and yet so little progress!" The box was a full-sized ship with a flat bottom and straight sides. It looked more like the big river transports that slowly moved food and other material down the larger rivers. Its lines were unbroken except for the large door and the windows at the top.

He saw the project foreman, Meta, reviewing plans and directing some men to the far end of the ship. He was waving to others to move some materials closer to the project. Noah saw his oldest son Japheth going into the project office, and his other sons, Shem and Ham, moving in that direction. Noah sighed and began to walk down the hill toward the front gate of the secured work area.

He walked past the guards at the gate, past the rows of transports, and to the door of the office, which slid open as he approached it.

"Good morning," he said to the woman at the table inside the door of the office.

"It's too early to be good," she snapped, without looking up.

Noah struggled with his emotions at her disrespect. As he studied her face, he reflected on how courtesy and respect had deteriorated so much over his lifetime. He thought about saying something to her, but decided to avoid an argument and not let her ruin his day.

"Welcome, Dad," Japheth said, as Noah entered the meeting room.

"Good morning," he answered in a rough voice. "And don't give me any trouble about it," he added quickly with a faint smile.

"I see our wonderful receiver has once again set her heart on taking the joy out of your day," Japheth, also smiling, responded.

"That woman is a disease," Ham said with disgust.

Noah shrugged. "I have to admit she isn't very pleasant to be around. But when was the last time we had someone in the office who had anything nice to say?"

Shem, pouring a drink for himself in the corner, said, "I think it was the last time Mother was here." Everyone but Ham laughed.

"I think we ought to get rid of this woman," said Ham.

"Mother?" Japheth asked with a grin.

"I don't think you're very funny," Ham said seriously.

"I think he is," said Shem as he sat down.

"I do, too," Noah agreed. "I think you're all funny. But I also think we'd better sit down and figure out how to move this project ahead even faster."

"I don't know if we can," Japheth said, sitting down. "We've already got so many workers that we can't make sure they're all working. And Meta's complaining about the quality of this new group that just came in."

"I agree with Dad," Shem said. "If we only have nine or ten months to finish this thing, we have to move it ahead faster. I don't see any way to get this done in time with the way we're going now."

"Dad," Japheth said slowly, "I think there's something that would help a lot."

"Go on," said Noah, settling deeper into his chair.

"Well," Japheth said, looking into his father's eyes, "I think if you spent more time here, it would make a big difference. I know your preaching work is important to you, but it takes you away from the work on the box. And everything moves twice as fast when you're here."

"I have to agree, Dad," said Shem.

Noah paused. "Thanks for your confidence, but you know I have to share the truth with as many people as I can."

Ham looked angry. "But what good has it done? Over a hundred years of preaching, and how many—besides us—have you gotten to listen?"

Noah was shocked by Ham's words. "It's not my job to make them listen," he answered, trying to control his anger. "It's my job to tell them what God expects and to warn them about what will happen if they don't stop sinning."

"Dad," Shem said, "I hate to admit it, but isn't Ham right? If you don't have a single person who believes you outside of our family, and this work really does need to be finished in ten months, shouldn't you make this a priority?"

Ham leaned forward. "In my last course at Upper School, the instructor said there's no point in preaching 'truth' to people, because truth is what each person thinks it is. I think he made a lot of sense."

"That's because you've spent thirty years at that den of stupidity," Japheth said sternly.

Ham's dark face was filled with fury. "Who do you think you are, calling my school a 'den of stupidity'? We're not the only family that knows anything. They have people up there who have over a hundred years of Upper School work to their credit. How can you spend that much time in school and not know something?"

"You ought to ask your instructor about that," Japheth retorted.

"Ham," Shem said with a grin, "when you get married next month, you're going to learn more in a year than you've learned your whole time in Upper School."

"Amen," Japheth added softly.

Ham spoke in a strained voice. "You two think you have all the answers, don't you? Well, I'm telling you that whatever truth we've learned as a family is meaningless to the rest of the world. They don't care about our truth. All they care about is good food, drink, and entertainment. They'd kill to keep those things, and they wouldn't trade a dead dog for our truth. So I say again that preaching isn't worth as much as getting this project done."

"Look," said Japheth, "I was the one who suggested that Dad spend more time here, but not because I think he's wrong in his preaching. There's only one truth, God's truth, and that's what he's preaching. I was just making a suggestion to move the project faster."

"I think we'd all better get on with our planning," Noah said sadly, as he made a note on the paper in front of him. "I spent so many years working for revival, before God finally made it clear that I had to begin work on the box," he said without looking up. "I have to admit that the preaching is so frustrating at times that I almost can't stand it."

There was a long pause, finally broken by the sound of the door opening behind Noah.

Meta stuck his head in the door. "Are you ready for me yet?" he asked in his gruff voice.

"Yes," Japheth answered. "Come in."

Meta, a large man of almost five cubits in height, looked younger than his age in his well-trimmed bodysuit. He went to the empty chair next to Shem, and roughed up Shem's short, dark-brown hair as he sat down. "I've never seen such terrible workers," Meta said abruptly.

"Are these even worse than the others?" Noah asked with a frown.

"Yes," Meta said disgustedly. "Workmanship gets poorer every year anyway, but I think we're getting more than our share of people who should be disintegrated."

Noah squirmed in his seat. "Please, Meta, let's keep our comments at a civilized level."

Meta looked down at his large, bony hands. "Send me some civilized workers, and I'll be civilized."

"Meta, you know —"

"All right," Meta said. "I'll watch what I say."

"Thank you," Noah responded. "Now, please give us your report."

"Well, the workers aren't very good. Some can't follow instructions, and most of them can't even read. But you know what the law says as well as I do — we've got to take whatever they send us."

"I know," said Noah. "Go on."

"Well, we're making good progress on the skeleton at the east end, in spite of the fact that I had to fire two workers yesterday. More material is due in tomorrow for two of the center sections. If our forming equipment holds up, we should be finished with that in about ninety days."

"That's too long," Shem protested. "We'll never get that area enclosed in time if we can't even get the skeleton done for three months!"

"Is there anything you can do to speed that up?" Noah asked.

"I'll do what I can," Meta nodded, still looking at his hands. "I'll need your clearance to fire three people who are really slowing the work down. And as for the woodwork on the south side of the ship . . ." He paused and looked up at Noah. "May I ask you a question?"

"Of course. But I've already told you why I'm building such a big ship," Noah added with a smile.

"It's not that," Meta said, avoiding Noah's smile. "I figure it's your business and your money, and you can spend it any way you want. But why do we have to use these antiquated designs? Why don't you have a powercenter, or at least sails? And all-metal ships bigger than this have been around for three or four hundred years. Why do we have to use gopher wood and all of this miserable pitch?"

Noah looked at Japheth, who had rolled back his large blue eyes, and then back at Meta. "That's a good question, Meta. Japheth asked me that question when he first saw the original drawings — almost nine years ago. I'll let him answer it."

Japheth looked surprised. "Well," he said slowly, "Dad gave me two reasons. First, and most important, he said God had told him to make it with gopher wood and pitch. God didn't say anything about powercenters or sails, so Dad left them out. I remember Dad saying, 'There'll be no place to go, so we won't need a way to get there.' And as far as the gopher wood and pitch are concerned, he said that the design, the weight, the flexibility, all would . . ." He stopped speaking and looked down.

"All would what?" Meta asked with interest.

"All would . . ." Japheth began, "all would work together to keep us safe when the flood comes."

"The *flood?*" Meta asked incredulously. "What's a *flood?*"

Noah saw that Japheth was struggling, so he answered instead. "The flood, Meta. You've seen men digging or cutting through rocks and hit a spring of water?" Meta nodded. "Well," Noah continued, "the flood's going to be like that. Only the flood is going to be the breakup of the whole earth. Everything—*everything,* Meta—is going to be destroyed, except for whoever and whatever gets on that ship.

"I think the water's going to come from every direction," Noah said, awe filling his voice. "Water's going to explode from beneath the earth, and the whole water canopy's going to come crashing down. That's one of the reasons that the ship is built like a chest or box, rather than like a normal ship. Its shape and length will make it almost impossible for it to be turned over when the huge waves come. With God's help, that big box should stay upright while the world is turned upside-down."

Meta sat back, dumbfounded. Noah had shared with him about God, but he had not yet told him about the terror that was coming, the terror beyond imagining.

"Incredible, isn't it, Meta?" Noah said gently, as he stroked his short black and white beard. "God hates sin, but He's slow to become angry. That's why most people think God's not there at all, or that He doesn't care about sin." Noah stood up and began walking back and forth. "But now, because of the incredible violence, He's angry, and He's coming to terrorize those who think that *they're* God. There's only one way out—to accept His coming serpent-slayer by faith, and then to get on that ship. There's no other exit, Meta."

Meta looked confused. "I've tried to be a good man," he said weakly. "I've followed most of the laws handed down from Adam."

Noah nodded. "I know, Meta, I know. You're different from most people. That's why I hired you. But being a good man and following God's law as well as you can isn't enough. You can't make up for your sin, and you can't be good enough to please a holy God. The only way is by faith in the coming serpent-slayer—the holy one who will rescue us from the evil one and bring an end to the curse of sin and death."

The room was quiet for several minutes. Finally, Meta stood up. "If there's nothing else, I'd better get back to work." Noah nodded and Meta left the room.

"He didn't understand at all," Ham said.

"I disagree," said Shem. "I think he understood what Dad was saying. I just don't think he accepted it."

"Same thing," Ham said sarcastically.

Shem shook his head. "Not at all, brother. He didn't just reject it. He's thinking about it. God will work on his heart. There's hope for that man."

"There's always hope," added Noah. "It's not our responsibility to make him believe, but just to offer him hope. Now it's between him and God."

"God help him," Japheth almost prayed.

Shem touched Japheth's hand. "God help us," he said.

CHAPTER 3

I t's the most ridiculous thing I've ever heard," the young man pacing
back and forth at the front of the room said with great frustration.
"It's the most ridiculous thing *anybody's* ever heard!"

Noah watched his nephew's face closely. Kenan was only 220, but
he tried to speak with the authority of a man two or three times his age.
He was a small man—only about three-and-a-half cubits—with black
eyes and thick, black hair. He spoke in a very loud, high-pitched voice
that he had always used to control conversations. His voice right now
was very loud and very high.

"Do you know what everyone's calling it, Uncle?" he demanded.
"Noah's folly! Noah's folly! Aghhh!" He looked down at Noah, who
was in a bodyrest next to Methusaleh. "Doesn't that tell you something?
Doesn't that make you *wonder?*"

"It does," said Noah cheerfully. "It makes me wonder how anyone
gets anything done with all the time they spend laughing at me."

"That's not what I mean," Kenan responded angrily.

"I know what you mean," Noah said seriously. "I know exactly
what you mean. People think I'm out of my mind. They think I should
be put in a mind treatment center. Some think I should be disintegrated."

"They just don't understand what you're trying to do," Methusaleh
said in a raspy voice.

"I don't either," said Naamah, Kenan's mother, as she came in from
the food preparation area. "Noah, people always respected you before,
even with all your preaching, because you were still at least . . ." She
stopped.

17

"Still at least what, dear sister?" Noah asked, his eyes dancing as he looked at her.

"Still at least—*normal*," she said. "Normal! But then you got the idea about that big wooden ship far from any water and changed all of our lives. People think we're out of our minds, too, just because we're related to you."

"At Upper School," Kenan said as he sat down, "people make up poems and songs about you, Uncle. They make up jokes about you."

"Tell me one," Noah said with interest.

"You're not serious," Kenan said with shock in his voice.

"I am. I'm totally serious. Tell me one."

"Well," Kenan began slowly, looking at his mother. "One learner came up to me today and asked if I knew why you were building this ship on land. When I told him no, do you know what he said? 'So he'll have a place to go after he's anchored his house in the harbor!'"

Noah hadn't intended to laugh, but he couldn't stop. He laughed until he cried. Kenan and Naamah stared at him, but Methusaleh finally joined in the laughter.

"I don't think it's funny at all," Naamah finally said in an angry tone. "You're embarrassing the family."

"Am I embarrassing you, Grandfather?" Noah asked, as he touched the old man on the arm.

Methusaleh shifted in his bodyrest. He had been a tall man, five-and-a-half cubits in height, but age and immobility had combined to make him seem smaller. Soft lines etched his face, although he had no marks of aging on his skin. His hair, a deep silver for as long as Noah could remember, was short, wavy, and neatly combed. His large, striking eyes peering out from under still-dark busy eyebrows, had always seemed to pierce Noah—eyes which remained unchanged from the early images of Methusaleh when he was a powerful, handsome young man. His smile had always been a warm sign to Noah. Methusaleh was smiling now.

"No, my son," Methusaleh answered. "I don't always understand you, and I don't always agree with you, but you've never embarrassed me once in your entire life. Your father—bless his memory—named you Noah, 'the comforter,' because he saw that you would be a comfort to him and to your family. You *are* a comfort to me. No, my dear grandson, you're not embarrassing me."

"Well," interjected Naamah as she walked over to Noah and pointed her finger at him, "you're embarrassing *me!* It's not just that stupid project—it's all of the preaching you do around the region. You've become much harder to listen to this last year. It's as though you think God's talking to you and you alone, like you've got some friendly relationship with God."

"I do," Noah said calmly, as he focused on his sister's cold, hardened face.

"You *are* in need of a mind treatment center, Uncle," Kenan said with genuine concern.

Noah looked up at his sister and suddenly remembered what a beautiful young woman she had been. Now, even with her efforts to look young and attractive, her face had become ugly, twisted, intimidating. He tried to think of her as his lovely big sister. He reached for her hand, but she pulled away.

"I remember when you used to be able to laugh, Naamah," he said gently. She glared at him, but he smiled at her. "You had a very special laugh," he added.

"I still laugh," she said, almost spitting the words. "I laugh at you. You're the biggest joke of my whole life."

Noah was stung by the words. "Your laugh used to be joyful and made everyone around you happy. Now it's a bitter laugh, Naamah, and it cuts those around you to pieces."

She started to speak, but looked at Methusaleh and then walked to the other end of the room, to the large window that overlooked Methusaleh's exquisite terraced garden. Noah looked at Kenan. "Kenan, how long have you been in Upper School?"

"Uh . . . about forty-five years."

"Do you have your approvals yet?"

"No, but I'm close," Kenan said defensively.

"What year will you get them?" Noah asked.

"Uh . . . if I keep going at my present pace . . . about 1665."

Noah stood up and walked over to the nearby window that overlooked the quiet pathway below. "My family," he said, still with his eyes focused on the sky, "there will *be* no 1665." He touched a press-point and tinted glass slid from left to right, darkening that part of the room around him. "This is the year 1655 after creation. You base your thinking on the idea that you'll have ten more years just like your last 220. But there will be no 1665!"

A long silence was broken by Methusaleh. "Noah, what are you saying? Are you really saying that God's going to destroy His entire creation?"

Noah looked at Methusaleh and then turned back to the window. "No, I'm not saying that at all. I think, even now, that God might spare this generation if there was real repentance. That's one of the hopes that keeps me preaching." He turned to face them, the bronze-tinted light outlining his five-cubit, broad-shouldered frame.

"But if there's no repentance?" Methusaleh asked.

Noah shook his head. "Then this world—not the earth itself, but this world as we know it—will be destroyed. The face of this earth is beautiful beyond compare, but it will be erased. And only those who get on that ship with me—and any ships like it that others might be building—will survive to start a new life on a new earth."

"Have you found these other shipbuilders, Uncle?" Kenan asked with obvious sarcasm.

"No, I haven't. But it doesn't matter. Even if we're the only ones, we're going to obey God."

"I can't stand to hear you talk about these things," Naamah said, as she walked back to the center of the room. Noah could see tears flowing down her cheek.

"I'm sorry I offend you," he said to her.

"You do offend me," she said as she fell into a bodyrest. She was still crying. "You talk about the destruction of our earth. Look out the window at the garden! Our world is so beautiful, so rich, so perfect. How can you talk about it all being . . . gone? Some people even think we're going to find Eden."

Noah walked toward her. "Even if they found Eden," he said, "they aren't fit to go in. Adam told us that these people want peace and perfection, but they want it *their* way. Men won't find their Edens until they find their God."

"We're going, Grandfather," Naamah said as she jumped up, went to Methusaleh, and kissed him on the forehead.

"Please, Naamah, one more thing," Noah said as he tried to hug her.

"No. No more," she said, pulling away from him. "I hate what you're doing to this family. And I . . . hate you."

"Stop!" Methusaleh shouted, sitting up in his chair. "Naamah, please ask your brother to forgive you."

"I won't!" she said as she ran out of the room. Kenan shook his head and walked out after her.

Noah walked to the bodyrest next to Methusaleh and sat down. "Grandfather, you're the patriarch of our family, the oldest living of our line. People will listen to you. You've watched things change so much since you were a little boy. Won't you help me warn those we love about the coming judgment?"

Methusaleh put his hand on Noah's face. "You're right when you say that things have changed greatly. Especially the violence. It's so terrible. Every night they show the molested and mutilated bodies of little children on the Reports." He dropped his arm. "But you can't even feel very sorry for those who are supposed to be helpless. Children curse and steal and kill. They hate anyone older than themselves, especially anyone in authority. Even little children are evil, horrible."

"I know what you mean," Noah said sadly. "I used to love spending time with children."

"And then there's the poor," Methusaleh continued. "You try to speak up for them, for the fours and fives, and then they band together and go on murderous rampages. They aren't innocent. *Nobody's* innocent. The changes for the worse in my 968 years leave me numb."

Noah took Methusaleh's aged hand in his own. "Then you agree?" he asked gently.

Methusaleh closed his eyes. "I just don't know. I see what you're saying—that God hates violence, that He's going to judge it—but it seems so unbelievable that He'd destroy the work of His own hands. He didn't even let them kill Cain after he committed the first murder—his own brother! That's why we don't take the life of murderers."

"And that, along with sin, is why we have so much murder!" Noah responded with conviction. "I hope in the world to come after the judgment by water that God will deal differently with murder and violence."

"But didn't God spare Cain?"

"Yes, He did. But don't you see? There was no one except close family living then. There was no government to bring justice. There was just Cain's family. God allowed Cain to live, but it wasn't because he didn't *deserve* to die. It was because God didn't want any family killing its wayward members."

"There's something you're forgetting, Noah," the old man said as he coughed. "You're forgetting that God is love. He's the creator, the one who *made* people. Don't you agree that God is love?"

"I do. But I think that's only part of His character. He's also holy. He's a lawgiver. He's a judge." Noah squeezed Methusaleh's hand. "I fear Him, Grandfather. I love Him, and I know that He loves me. But I fear Him. Once He decides on judgment, no man, no generation can resist Him."

Methusaleh patted Noah on the leg. "Are you saying that God made a mistake with man?"

Noah sighed. "No. I'm saying that *man* made a mistake with *God.* He could have made us without choice. But we both know, Grandfather, that there's no joy in love if someone *has* to love you. The love that brings joy is the love that's given freely. He made us with choice. Cain made the wrong choice. All these years later, almost *everyone* is making the wrong choice. Wrong choices bring hard results."

They sat for a long time, each one lost in his thoughts.

"Don't let life make you hard, Noah," Methusaleh finally said.

"I *am* hard toward life," Noah said firmly. "I want to be soft toward God and hard toward all the things that would tear me down. If I listen to these voices, I'll forget my good fear of God and I'll stop building that ship. That's when I'll really be in trouble."

"But, my . . ." Methusaleh's voice trailed off as the sound of voices arguing could be heard in the entryway.

"I'll find out what it is," Noah said as he stood up.

At that moment the door slid open and Shem came running into the room. At once Noah could see that his son had been beaten. "What happened?" he asked in dismay.

"It's the packs," Shem moaned as he fell into a bodyrest. He put a cloth on his mouth to stop the bleeding. "It's those packs that have been destroying things all over the old part of the city. Everyone was gone but Ham and I and about a dozen workers when they came."

"I hate it," Methusaleh said with tears.

Noah got some water in a pan and brought it to his son. As Shem began to wash his face, Noah walked back to the window and looked at the setting sun. He closed his eyes.

"Now it begins," he said in a whisper. "Please help me, God."

CHAPTER 4

From the top of the hill, Noah looked down on turmoil and confusion. He stood, unable to move, trying to take in the enormity of what had happened.

In the work area to the north of the ship, several healing units had arrived. Several men were loading some of the injured into the units. He saw Japheth helping one man to a temporary bodyrest next to a healing unit that was just backing in. Noah looked back and forth, trying to see the unmistakable modern sign of death — the dark red containers that would be filled with the dead and shipped to the Regional Determination Center.

He breathed with relief as he saw no evidence of death — neither the dreaded red containers nor the vulture-like organ-recovery units. He lifted his right arm to heaven and praised God for delivering his project from death and for protecting his sons from harm.

As he began to walk down the hill, he could see that several pieces of equipment had been damaged. He tried to remember if there were any spare parts for this equipment in his underground storage chamber. But before he could finish his thoughts, he saw something that made him stop in his tracks.

The ship itself had been damaged, although not badly enough to stop the project. The enemy had not gotten higher than the first level, and the second and third levels appeared to be untouched. But the worst for Noah was what he saw on the side of the ship.

There, written in letters as tall as a man, were horrible words blaspheming God. He had heard these words in the city, and even there they had made him feel sick and angry. But here—written on the ship planned for and designed by God—were these same words, attacking the very God whom Noah knew and loved and worshiped.

Noah slumped to the ground.

It was several minutes before he heard a voice. "Dad?" he heard Japheth saying next to him. "Dad? Are you all right?"

Finally Noah looked up at him. There was his oldest son—tall and muscular, but with the neatly trimmed beard and moderately long hair that made him look like one of the thinkers from the Upper School. "Yes, Japheth," Noah responded weakly, "I'm all right."

Japheth sat down next to him. "I suppose we've expected this kind of thing for a long time, but it's still a shock when it happens. I hope it's not the start of something."

"Tell me . . . tell me what happened," Noah said, still looking at the ship.

"It was one of those packs from the city," Japheth answered, also looking at the ship while he spoke. "It was one of the 'skinhead' groups. They came from nowhere and were in the work area in front of the ship before anyone realized what was happening. I was on the upper level and couldn't get down because the power-lift operator ran when he saw them coming. So all I could do was watch."

"That had to be terrible," Noah said with a sigh.

"Worse than that," Japheth said, his anger rising. "They came in and just started beating people, hitting them with anything they could find on the ground. They were screaming and cursing. If someone resisted, they gathered around him and really hurt him. They began kicking and beating the equipment. Except for the forming units, though, they didn't do much damage. They were just too wild and unfocused."

"And it wasn't just enough that they had to do that," Noah quietly added. "They also had to insult God."

"Their laughing was demonic," Japheth remembered, shuddering. "They took such delight in it—it's still hard for me to believe that anyone can be that degenerate. I tried praying for them, but . . . well, it was hard praying with all the laughing and cursing. I just wanted to strike them down!"

"Their time will come," Noah said in hushed tones. "Their time will come, and they can't escape. They think they can mock God, but their laughter will stop forever the day that God changes the face of this earth." He leaned back on his hands and looked up to the sky. "You don't have to strike them, Japheth. God will do it with His own arm."

"That's how I ended up praying," Japheth said as he looked at the city. "I couldn't pray for God's blessing on them, and even praying for them to change at that moment seemed . . . out of place. I just prayed that God would deal with them, judge them, strike them down. I hated what they were doing to people and what they were saying about God."

"A time can come for that kind of praying," Noah agreed. "I didn't think so when I was younger. But once people go past sin and evil to spitting in God's face . . ." Noah closed his eyes.

"I have some other news for you before you go down," Japheth said after a pause. He turned to face Noah and crossed his legs in front of him. He began to sweep the rich grass with his right hand. "Ham left this morning. We had a . . . discussion about the project, and he got angry and went into the city. I think he was going to meet with some of his friends."

"His 'friends,'" Noah muttered. "Someday he's going to discover who his real friends are." He shook his head. "Sometimes I think one of the biggest problems we have is knowing who our real friends are and treating them as they deserve. It's too easy to take them for granted — even while we bow down to those who really don't care about our hearts and lives."

After a brief silence, Japheth touched his father's arm. "One thing I know is this: You're my true friend, as well as my father. I hope I never take you for granted. Sicilee feels the same way."

Noah smiled at him.

"You two are very special. I felt from the beginning that God had brought you a wife that would stand up for God in this unholy age."

"Dad," Japheth said hesitantly, "do you want me to look for Ham?"

"No. I don't think so. But a time may come when we have to rescue him. He just hasn't grasped the idea that he can't be a friend to people who live like that, and still be God's friend."

They sat together looking at the city. Noah squinted his eyes, as though somehow he might be able to see his youngest son.

"Let's go," Noah said finally as he jumped to his feet. "I want to hear Meta's report."

Noah helped Japheth to his feet, and together they walked down the hill. "I don't like the look on Meta's face," Noah said.

"I don't either," Japheth agreed. "He looks angrier than the 'skinheads.'"

Noah came alongside Meta, who was shouting directions to someone on the second level. The words he was using made Noah cringe.

Meta turned his head. When he saw Noah, he stopped his shouting in the middle of a command. "Sorry, sir," he said, respectfully. "I'm just so angry that I could . . ."

"I know," Noah agreed. "I could, too. How does it look?"

"Not too bad with the project itself. I think we could get back on schedule in three or four days. But not with the other problem."

"What's that?"

"Many people are leaving their work," Meta said with disgust. "Dogs!" he exploded suddenly, spitting on the ground. He saw Noah look at him with disappointment. "I'm sorry, but I've seen dogs who have more ability and courage than some of these. It's actually a compliment to call them 'dogs.'"

Noah was smiling. "You know I'm not going to accept *that* explanation."

Meta kicked at a piece of broken wood. "I know," he said with a grudging smile. "But it's the way I feel. A little trouble, and they want to leave! Nobody even got killed. Some of these people spend their time off in places that are much more dangerous than this project. One of them got killed in a fight at one of those drug centers just last week."

Noah looked at the angry manager. He guessed that Meta was about 450 years old. *This man has seen so much violence in his lifetime,* Noah thought to himself. *Too much.*

"How many are we losing?" Japheth asked from the other side of Meta.

"About half," Meta said in his gruff voice. "It'll take me about three weeks to get back up to full force."

Noah shook his head. "It won't work. We need to get back up to full force faster than that. Increase the wages if you have to."

"Increase the wages!" Meta was outraged. "For these dogs?"

"I know," Noah responded gently. "But Meta, even dogs get to eat." Meta grunted his acceptance of the order and walked over to where some men were standing and arguing.

"I'd hate to be them," Japheth whispered.

"Me, too," Noah agreed.

"Dad, you know we'll have trouble with the regional government over this, don't you?"

Noah nodded slowly. "Yes, I do. They can't stop the violence, but they can tie up a lot of our time talking about it."

"Have you thought about what we'll do when we get to . . . the other side?"

Noah grimaced. "I have. Parents with their children, spiritual leaders with their followers, governments with their citizens—we have to train people to know that discipline based on God's standards *has* to be done or everything will eventually die. Spiritual leaders—starting with you and me, Japheth—have to teach people about the terrible fruit of rebellion against God."

Japheth nodded in agreement. "I know people who complain that the government is letting people be out of control, and at the same time they let their own children do anything they want and never interfere with their sin."

"That's where the problems begin," Noah said, putting his hand on Japheth's shoulder. "Big problems start in little places called 'homes.'" He hugged Japheth. "I'm going to remind you of that when you have children."

"Please do," Japheth said with emotion. "I think," he said after a pause, "I'd better get down to the healing center and make arrangements to pay for our people's care." Noah nodded and Japheth went to his transport.

Noah began to walk slowly around the project. *So much to be done,* he thought. He made mental calculations as he looked at the damage and the blasphemy. Just as he pulled a voice recorder out of his pocket, an airship streaked overhead, tipping its wings as it turned toward the airdock at the eastern edge of the city.

"Lord," he said out loud, "why do I have to use such crude materials? Why can't I use everything available to build this ship? Why can't I use anything but this wood and pitch?"

He stopped walking. He had that same kind of strong inward thought that had stopped him years before and told him to build the ship. The thought then was unmistakable, and this thought was the same. He had never heard God speak to him in an audible voice, but he knew that this thought had come into his heart directly from God.

Friend, the thought came, *you have to do it this way because I say so. You were the one whose heart was turned to me. At first, you were the only one. The only one to obey me, the only one to do things just because I say so. That's why, at the appointed time, you're going to get on that ship with your family and live. I won't let you use these things that man has made for himself in these later years when his heart turned from Me. They're a stench to Me, even as man glories in his accomplishments. Others may use those things, My true son — but you may not.*

Noah stood in the same place for a long time, looking up at the sky. He squinted, as though he was trying to see the One who was speaking. "Note to Meta," he finally said into the voice recorder. "Before anything else, get rid of that blasphemy."

Noah looked up at the sky again, and smiled.

CHAPTER 5

Noah and Tess looked through the window of the little eatinghouse as they waited for their food to be served.

"Look at those new clothes," Tess whispered to Noah as she nodded across the busy greenspace. Noah followed her direction and saw the group she was watching.

The two women in the group were dressed in the new bodysuits that Noah had only seen on signs before. The tops exposed their backs and the lower part fit tightly around each leg. The colors were a mixture of purples, yellows, and greens. The women's hair was combed to look wild and out of control. The men were in the traditional trim bodycovers, but they were tighter than usual. As one of the men turned, Tess looked away.

"Terrible," Noah said as he watched Tess's eyes move from the scene outside. "You can see a day coming when they won't be wearing anything at all."

"That's when I stop coming to the city and just have them deliver things to our home," Tess responded.

"You'll still have to worry about the person who delivers," Noah reminded her. He watched the server as she placed their food — a huge plate of steamed and grilled vegetables — before them. "Thank you," he said softly. The woman frowned at him and walked away. "I think she liked me," he whispered to Tess. She caught his eyes and they both burst into laughter.

"I think it's your charm," she added, causing another round of laughter.

Noah prayed for God's blessing on their day and for the people outside the window. They ate their meal slowly while they discussed Ham's interest in being close to those who didn't share their values. "Sometimes," Noah said with concern, "I'm not even sure he'll get on that ship with us."

Tess nodded to show her agreement. "I share that concern, but he does know the truth."

"I just hope he *loves* the truth enough to obey it," Noah responded as he took a bite.

"He's always come around," Tess said defensively, as she sliced a piece of cheese from a block in the middle of the table, "and I think Nusheela's going to be a good wife for him. He's been the most difficult, but I think he's going to make the right decisions."

"I hope you're right," Noah responded seriously. "I pray that you're right." He took her hand into both of his. "You usually are," he said gently.

"I had a long talk this morning with Kedrah," Tess said, taking a bite of cheese.

"How is she doing?" Noah asked with interest.

"Not too well. It's just so frustrating! We talk about God, and she really gets excited. She really likes talking about spiritual things. But her husband is just so . . ."

"Careful," he teased.

"I know, I know," she said, smiling. "I know we're supposed to be kind with our words, but he's just such a . . . goat!"

"A goat?" Noah said, trying to control his laughter. "A *goat?*"

"Yes, a goat," she said briskly. "He bumps into her life every day. Just about the time she starts getting close to God, he knocks her down. She told me just a few weeks ago that she was falling in love with God all over again. It didn't take him long to change that."

Noah leaned back and sighed. "I think it's worse because he appears to be a man who's also interested in spiritual things."

"It is worse," Tess agreed. "Please pray for her. I don't know what he's going to do, but I love her so much and I want her to get on the box with us."

After Noah prayed, they finished their meal and went to the exit. Noah handed the record of expense to the woman at the door and placed his right hand under the hand-line reader. As the woman entered the record, a light came on and scanned Noah's hand. He smiled at the woman and hurried out the door with Tess.

"Why are you hurrying so?" she asked in surprise.

"I couldn't take another frown," he said. He looked at Tess and smiled. "I suppose I'm getting a little sensitive in my middle age."

"You're not that old," she responded, poking him in the side.

As they turned to their right to go toward the market exchange, they could see a group of men coming toward them. When they were about fifty cubits away, Noah realized who was leading them.

"Pray quickly, Tess," he urged. "It's Mizraim."

The men quickly surrounded Noah and Tess, blocking the walkway and causing the heavy flow of people to go around them. Mizraim came up to Tess and bowed.

He was very tall and extremely muscular. His hands were the biggest Noah had seen except for the Nephilim. Mizraim's face was considered very handsome by most people, and that — along with his incredible wealth — had brought him twelve wives, plus fourteen others whom he had set aside. His eyes were gloomy and depressing, but his smile was engaging and warm. Although he was Noah's age, he looked a hundred years younger.

"You're a lovely woman," he said to Tess while his unlit eyes looked her over. "Too lovely for this fool here," he added, never taking his eyes off her.

Noah saw Tess's face contort with anger, but she said nothing.

"People," Mizraim shouted to those passing by, "don't you think this woman is too lovely to be in covenant with this fool?" Some people began to gather around the circle of men. "People," Mizraim continued, "isn't it a great sadness that a woman of such character would have to live with a man who should be in a mind treatment center, a man who builds a ship where there is no water?" The crowd began to laugh.

It was too much for Tess. "There are fourteen women who would have done better covenanting with him rather than you!" she said, her voice strained.

Mizraim smiled at her. "Ah, the woman has spirit!" He finally looked at Noah. "You're a dog," Mizraim said with disdain. "You don't deserve such a woman." The men behind Noah began to growl and bark in his ear. "Dog!" they said to him over and over.

Mizraim moved closer to Tess. "Leave this dog," he said, in a strangely charming way. "Leave this dog, and come to me," he added as he put his hand on her arm.

"I've lived with this man for almost three hundred years," she answered, pulling away. "I'd rather die with him than spend an hour with you!" Mizraim frowned, and the men around them became silent.

Noah knew it was time to speak. "Mizraim," he began slowly, "Mizraim. Why does a man of such importance bother with someone he thinks is a dog?"

Mizraim turned to face Noah. He stared into Noah's eyes. "Because," he said with great hatred, "you're a dog who won't stay in his place. You speak to others, so they can become dogs, too." The men behind Noah began to growl and bark again.

"It seems by the sound of them," said Noah, "that many of your men must be my followers."

The crowd around the circle exploded into laughter, and the men behind Noah became silent again. Mizraim's face darkened with anger. Noah could almost feel the presence of evil spirits.

"We're going to leave now," Noah tensely whispered. "You've had your enjoyment, and now we're going to leave."

Mizraim stepped in front of Noah. "You won't go until I say so," he hissed. "Do you think you can make a fool of me?"

Noah smiled. "I have nothing to do with that. What you are, you've made yourself." Several people in the crowd laughed, but quickly stopped as they saw Mizraim looking at them.

Mizraim began to pace around the small space. "The great Noah," he said sarcastically. "The great Noah! Here's a man who built an empire, a man who has more wealth than most men even dream about. But is he happy with that? No! He begins to fill our city, our entire region, with his nonsense about God. And then one day, he wakes up and starts to build a ship—a ship where there's no water! He uses up our resources, because his God tells him a judgment is coming. No one says

anything to him, because he's a man of great reputation, because he says
he helps people."

Mizraim stopped in front of Noah. "But I spit on your reputation!
Your ship is an ugly reminder about an ugly god of legend, a god who
makes people and then kills them. Your ship makes people laugh, but it
also makes them discouraged and sick inside. Your preaching was bad
enough, but *you* could at least be ignored. That contemptible ship is too
big to be ignored."

Noah smiled again. "Maybe that's why God made it so big."

Mizraim laughed scornfully. "God, God. I've never seen this God.
I'm almost 600 years old, and I've never seen this God."

"You will," Noah responded. "Mizraim, you *will* see this God. And
when He holds you over the pit, what will you say to Him then?" Noah
looked out at the crowd. "Men and women, you know me and know that
I've done none of you any harm. Do you think this is right, that a man
with a pack can keep one man and one woman from leaving if they
choose?"

"I think they can keep you," a man shouted from the crowd, "because you're scum!" Several voices added their agreement. The men in
Mizraim's pack started chanting "Noah's scum, Noah's scum."

Noah quickly decided on a different approach. "Mizraim, I thought
you were a brave leader. What courage does it take to surround a man
and his wife? Why would you ruin your reputation by an attack on us?"
Noah prayed that God would provide an escape.

At that moment, a commander forced his way into the open space.
He looked at Noah and then at Mizraim. "Is this man bothering you?"
he asked Mizraim.

"He bothers me very much," Mizraim said, his eyes still on Noah.
"But he's a dog. I'm not going to let a dog make me angry." Mizraim
turned and walked away, and his surprised men began to follow after
him.

"Move along," the commander said gruffly to the crowd, "before I
have to break some heads." He looked at Noah. "I'd especially like to
break your head. Move!" Noah grabbed Tess's arm and walked away,
shaking his head.

                          ❧ ❧ ❧

As they sped along the pathway home, Tess realized that her husband hadn't spoken since they left the market exchange. "Hey, friend," she said softly, "what are you thinking?"

"Well," he said slowly, "I was thinking about the time with Mizraim. Why can't he just leave us alone?"

She put her hand on his arm. "When I asked you that question about some other people long ago, you told me that anyone who serves God can expect to be attacked and treated with disrespect." He looked at her and saw her smiling.

"You know," he said in a more relaxed tone, "sometimes I think it'd be much easier to serve God if I didn't have to deal with people."

"Does that include me?" she asked in a playful voice.

He patted her leg. "No. It would be *harder* to serve God if I didn't have you to help."

"I don't think the people in the market exchange helped your feelings when they wouldn't turn off that violent viewing when you asked them."

"I still can't believe it." He shook his head. "Someone is being killed, and they make an image of it for entertainment! People live a whole lifetime and they're murdered, and other people clap their hands. When I see something like that, it makes me believe that God's judgment can't be far away and that maybe I'm not out of my mind."

"I can't believe that others haven't accepted your message yet," Tess said to encourage him.

"I think that's the hardest part. The world is bad, people are bad, our unseen enemies are bad. But if there were just a few others, a few outside our family who . . ." After a pause, he continued. "That's the hardest, Tess. After all of my preaching, I'm not sure anyone else will join us." He seemed to sag.

"What about Methusaleh?" she asked.

"I don't . . . I don't know. He listens, sometimes he even agrees, but . . . but he won't make a commitment. He says, 'I'm too old and useless. What can I do? I think I should just die and get out of the way.'"

"I hate that," Tess said, anger rising in her voice. "I hate that so much. We've made old people feel so worthless, just because they can't do what they used to do. Some of them could even do more, but they've been so discouraged."

"I'll talk to him again," Noah agreed.

"I'll pray for you," she answered, squeezing his hand. "And Kedrah and Meta. Those two could come with us. We just can't stop trying."

As they passed through the mountain walls that led to their home, Noah remembered his father's dying words. "Comforter," his father had said to him, "God has shown me that punishment is coming because of the sin of Cain. But you can escape. Take others with you if you can, but you obey our God and escape!" His father had pulled him close to whisper in his ear. "There may only be a few. But don't count on numbers. Count on your God!"

It's you and me, God, he prayed silently.

As they came over a hill they could see the exquisite sunset. Then he looked over at Tess. *You and me and her,* he corrected himself.

CHAPTER 6

GREEN VEGETABLES BY KIND," the words stared back at him. As he looked at the image, Noah felt numb. He had been working on calculations for food and seed for several hours. He wanted to stop, but felt pressure to finish the list so he could give it to Japheth after the midday meal.

The numbers were staggering. He had known for months what he felt should have been obvious to him from the beginning—that if all men were going to be destroyed, all animals were going to be destroyed, too. If God wanted animals in the world to come, Noah was going to have to take them on the ship.

The thought had come to him suddenly while he was resting on a Sabbath. Until then he had thought that the ship was to be so large because of the great numbers of people who would be joining them. He had hoped that hundreds of people would repent, accept the coming serpent-slayer, and share in this journey to a changed earth.

But he had come to realize after years of preaching that few people were willing to listen. Only Tess and Japheth and Shem had committed themselves fully to the work. Ham and Methusaleh went back and forth in their thinking. None of his sons' wives had as yet said they would step on the ship at the appointed time.

So on that Sabbath Noah had been asking God about the size of the ship. And God had told him clearly, inside his spirit, that there would be few people—but many animals.

And Noah had to bring the food to feed them all.

Noah now understood that the ship was intended by God to be a self-contained world of its own. Everything needed for life was to be on it—food, seed, clothes, knowledge, people, plants, animals. Anything forgotten, anything not on the ship when the judgment came, would be gone forever, buried in the raging flood.

The thought made Noah tremble and work even harder on his planning. Into the night he would read books about farming and plant life. He asked God to help him not to forget the tiniest flower. Tess had once teased him about leaving behind his least favorite vegetables. He had bought seed for them first.

Noah had not yet shared these insights with his family. Except for Tess, none of them had a clear idea of how great the destruction of the earth would be, how nothing could survive unless it was on a ship like his. None of them had talked with him about animals or food or seed. They, like he, had assumed that the ship was being built to hold the crowds that would come as their hearts were pierced.

Noah was not looking forward to conversation with his sons and their wives about animals and what would be required in the way of food and work. Their family had not been involved in farming for hundreds of years. They had worked instead in the advancement of systematic knowledge and its practical applications and had lived in cities since the Great Northern War of 1172 A.C.. For now, Noah decided to keep this new insight to himself.

A newer thought was so overwhelming to him that he had decided not to tell his family until after the flood, when he could verify it for himself. Most of the men of knowledge were in agreement that the length of people's lives was directly related to two things and without them, lives would be much shorter. The first was the incredible richness of the soil. The second was the protection from the sun provided by the water canopy. Just days before, Noah had realized that both of these things could be gone forever in the new earth.

As he touched a presspoint to change images, Tess knocked and came into the room. The door slid closed behind her.

"Yes?" he said, a little harshly.

"I'm sorry," she said quickly, and turned to leave the room.

He had never handled interruptions as well as he would have wished, and watching her reaction made him realize that he'd missed his opportunity again. "Come here, little girl," he said with affection. He stood up and gave her a hug. "Maybe if I live to be 700, I'll learn to handle these simple situations better."

"I know you're under a lot of stress," she said weakly.

"Not *that* much," he responded. "Never that much." He held her close and asked, "Is midday meal ready?"

"Almost. But that's not why I came up. A building reviewer just let me know that he'll be here in less than an hour to review the project with you."

"Oh no!" Noah said with dismay. "Those people are . . . why today, with the preaching I need to do tonight?"

"The enemy has many tools," Tess chided softly.

Noah took her hand and walked down to the first level. As they reached the bottom of the stairs, Noah looked through the stained glass panel at the side of the door and saw the building reviewer and his enforcers walking across the greenspace toward the house.

"You go to the back room," he said to Tess. "One of us having to deal with these people is enough."

She nodded in agreement. "Kedrah's coming over in a few minutes. Let's be in prayer for each other while we're in the middle of these spiritual wars."

He kissed her and walked outside to meet the visitors. "Greetings!" he said, more cheerfully than he felt.

"We're here to see the . . . project," the reviewer growled.

"Can I offer you something to drink?"

"No," the man answered viciously. "Are you trying to bribe me?"

Noah had dealt with this before. "No," he said calmly. "I'm trying to offer you a drink. But I suppose you can do your review just as well thirsty as not, so let's go."

Noah got into his transport and led the group toward the work area and the project. Passing through the gate, Noah got out and waited for them to catch up. When they were close, he started walking. He could hear the enforcers behind him whispering and laughing.

The reviewer came alongside him, looking at some notes. "I see here that you've had many recent injuries. Do you have any explanation?"

Noah prayed to remain calm. "Yes, I have an explanation. We had one of the packs come and attack our project and workers. No one's been injured because of the work itself in over three months. We have guards, but no one can defend a project from an attack by a large pack."

"Are you aware," the man droned, "that under Article 17 of the Building Statutes, you as the owner are responsible for every injury on your project, no matter what the cause is?"

Noah felt the frustration welling up inside him. "Are you serious? You're saying that you can interpret that statute to make me responsible for *anything* that happens to these people?"

"I can interpret it in any way I want," the man answered smugly. "The Mastermen have given me complete authority in these things."

"What if one of the workers kills another worker in anger?"

"If it happened on your project, you'd be responsible—at least in my region."

Noah was angry. "Who do you think you . . ."

"Careful," one of the enforcers said. "If you touch him, you'll be dead."

The reviewer began laughing as they got closer to the ship. "I'd heard about 'Noah's folly,' but you really do have to see it to appreciate it." He held up his voice recorder and began to speak. "Twenty-two serious injuries, result of owner's negligence; forty-five thousand. Using gopher wood and pitch"—he stopped to laugh—"twenty-five thousand. Antiquated specifications; thirty thousand. Building project in wrong location"—he grinned at Noah—"fifteen thousand." He touched a press-point on the side of the recorder. "The fine will be one hundred and fifteen thousand darmas."

Noah felt faint. The fine amounted to almost a tenth of his total wealth. "One hundred and fifteen thousand?" he asked in disbelief. "Where do you think people get that kind of money?"

"That's your problem," the man said coldly. "And there's more. I'm going to increase your requirements for assurance by half." He looked at Noah with disdain. "And I'll tell you this: I'd like to shut this project down today. If you have any more injuries, I *will* shut it down, and you have no appeal. If I shut it down and you continue to build, my men here"—he waved his hand toward the enforcers—"my men here will, how should I say, *encourage* you in a different direction."

Noah felt intimidated but also felt pressure from his God to say something. He had learned long ago to yield to the pressure from God and avoid having to ask God's forgiveness for lost opportunity—and also avoid having to find the person to share it in the end anyway. It was hard saying it now, but it was easier than saying it later. "The day will come when you won't laugh at that ship," he said confidently.

"What?"

"If I'm building this ship on my own, not because of God, then you're right and I'm out of my mind. I deserve to be treated as you are treating me. But if I'm building this ship to escape God's coming wrath, and you live to see that wrath, then that will be the day you stop laughing at me—and stop laughing at God."

"The people at the central office said you were obsessed and strange," the reviewer said. "They said you'd talk a lot about God and other sick things. But I don't have to listen to this."

Noah started to respond but now felt the pressure to hold his words and not give God's truth to a man who was mocking God. "You're right," he said quietly. "You don't have to listen to this." He watched them walk back to their transport and leave. He then walked to his own transport and got in. He couldn't move for almost an hour.

ﻚ ﻚ ﻚ

Shortly after Noah had left with the reviewer, Tess heard Kedrah's knock at the door.

"Greetings, friend!" Tess said as the door slid open.

"Hello, Tess," Kedrah said, avoiding eye contact.

"Come in and sit down," Tess encouraged, leading the way into the spacious greeting room. "Something cool to drink?" she asked as Kedrah took her seat. Tess held out a glass of cool nectar. Kedrah took it and quickly began sipping it.

Kedrah was a beautiful woman about half Tess's age. She had long blonde hair and a rounded face with a spray of light freckles. She had big blue eyes, a delicate nose, and a small mouth. Without apparent effort, she maintained a youthful figure. On several occasions she had shared with Tess how her good looks had gotten her involved as a young person in several wrong relationships with men.

"So how are you today?" Tess asked with sincere interest.

"Not so good," Kedrah answered sadly. "I just can't . . . well, you know."

"It's Pelenah again?" Tess asked.

"Yes." Kedrah put the glass down. "It's just so hard, Tess. One day he seems to care about me and God. The next day he doesn't seem to care at all. I keep thinking it's my fault, but I just don't know what I could be doing to cause it."

Tess nodded knowingly. "Dear one, you're not the first woman to deal with this. All through the years women who have wanted to get ahead spiritually have felt held back by husbands who seemed hot one day and cold the next. If you're right with God, it isn't your fault; it's your husband not choosing to be right with God."

"But what am I supposed to do?" Kedrah asked with great discouragement.

"Keep moving ahead with God," Tess answered simply.

Kedrah shook her head. "That's easy to say because you're married to a real man of God. But it's not so easy to live with a man like Pelenah. I love him and I want to please him. And you've told me many times that I have to be under his authority."

"I have," Tess agreed. "But that doesn't mean that you let him drag you down or keep you away from God. Pelenah isn't God. You're always under the one true God first, and Pelenah as he gives you godly direction. You don't have to follow him—you *must* not follow him— when he tells you to go away from God."

"Are you sure?" Kedrah asked, confusion filling her voice. "One older woman who goes to our God-house told me that you always have to obey your husband, no matter what. Even if he tells you to sell yourself or commit some other sin, you have to do it to be right with God."

"Terrible!" Tess almost shouted. "That's just terrible. She's saying her husband is God. Husbands can be wonderful partners in life and great leaders, Kedrah, but they make very poor gods."

"Oh, I guess I know that," Kedrah sighed. "I knew that wasn't right. But I'm still uncomfortable going to God-house without him. I don't even feel comfortable—I have to say this—inviting you and Noah over. I just know it would create tension."

Tess moved close to her. "What are you afraid of, Kedrah?"

"I'm not sure," Kedrah answered sadly. "I think I'm just afraid of getting ahead of my husband spiritually. It just doesn't seem right. It seems like I have to stop and wait for him."

"Don't do that," Tess pleaded. "That won't help him. Kedrah, you've been learning some wonderful things about God. Please keep learning and applying those things in your life. As you grow in your knowledge and love of God, you'll have more of value in your life to share with your husband. But even if he never listens, you can get closer to God."

"And then . . ." Kedrah stopped.

"And then what?" Tess encouraged.

"And if I really get closer to God, you're going to say I have to leave my husband and get on that ship."

Tess felt great compassion for her friend. "Dear, I know how this is tearing at your heart. I suppose you could accept the serpent-slayer as your defender and still not get on the box. But if you really give Him control over your life, I don't know why you wouldn't want to get on— not even if that meant leaving an unbelieving husband behind."

Kedrah was crying. "He's still my husband," she said pathetically.

"I know that," Tess responded. "I know that. I'm not telling you to set him aside. That would be wrong. But I'm saying again that you can't let him keep you from God. And Kedrah, it's not as though you're going to have any life with Pelenah if you stay. This world is coming to an end. You don't want to be swept away in God's judgment, do you?"

"No, no," Kedrah moaned. "But I don't want to leave my husband behind either. Can't you understand that, Tess?"

"I *do* understand that, friend," Tess said softly. "You may be facing a very tough choice. I want to pray for you now, that you'll make the right one."

"Thank you, Tess," Kedrah said as she hugged her. "I think with your help, I *will* be able to make the right choice."

 ❧ ❧ ❧

"How was it?" Tess asked as Noah walked in.

"It was like having endday meal with a leviathan, and the food is gone, but he still looks hungry—and then he looks at you."

Tess laughed and hugged him. "That bad?"

"That bad. But I don't want to talk about the details right now. I will tell you, though, that we need to pray for money to finish this project." He squeezed her close to him. "I know now why God let me gather so much wealth. He knew how much it was going to take to get it done."

"Let's do pray," Tess agreed. "And let's add Kedrah to our prayers. She's so torn between Pelenah and God. She doesn't see that having Pelenah and not God is the same as having nothing."

"So much work to do," Noah said with a sigh. "But the most important work this night is prayer. I'll pray for the project and then I'll agree with you while you pray for your friend Kedrah."

 ❧ ❧ ❧

Sometime later, as the evening shadows fell into the area inside the door, Japheth came to wish his father well on his preaching later that evening. He looked through the window and saw his father and mother hugging. He could see his mother's lips moving in the fading light.

The young man sat down outside the door, and joined his parents in prayer.

CHAPTER 7

T he man grabbed either side of the speechtable with his hands. "Friends," he said in a ringing voice, "we have a special speaker here with us tonight. Most of you have heard of Noah Seth-Lamech. But let me give you some of the details of his life . . ."

Noah's thoughts began to wander as the speaker, his friend for over five hundred years, gave the listeners the details of Noah's life. Noah looked around the God-house and tried to take in the size and the beauty of the building.

One of the three largest God-houses in the entire region, almost ten thousand people could be seated inside. The glasslights were enormous; Noah took the time to count them and could see sixteen from his seat behind the speaker. The workmanship on the finished wood was intricate and flawless. Huge paintings with special lighting hung on every available wall.

One old painting near the front caught his attention. It depicted the scene in the Garden of Eden after Adam had sinned. Its realism was stunning. Eve was on the right, lying on the ground, her head on her arms, obviously weeping. She was looking away from the scene at the center. In the center was Adam, on his knees, his hands folded, his head bowed. He looked strikingly young and vigorous.

But the third figure in the painting was the one that arrested Noah's attention. It was a man dressed in a shining, white robe. His face was dark, framed by short black hair and a black, short-trimmed beard. The face was rugged and strong. The man was standing over Adam, almost leaning toward him. Noah was pierced as he saw how gently the man held Adam's face in His hands.

Noah looked again at the room as a whole. Although Noah's desire for things to be done well was strong, he was appalled at the waste he saw in the building—such a waste to spend so much on a God-house when there were millions of people living in unimaginable poverty. He sighed as he realized what a shame it was to spend so much on a building in which truth was seldom or never preached anymore. And then he thought of the irony of spending so much, when all of the beauty and wealth was going to be swept away in an instant by God's coming judgment.

But tonight, Noah told himself, *it doesn't have to be a waste.* He thought about all of his preaching for the past 120 years and knew that God would be present to encourage him. Tonight, with God's help, Noah purposed to make truth resound from the walls.

". . . came here and built a business that at its peak gave work to over four thousand people. As you know, he also contributed to many . . ."

Noah began to study the listeners. It was a wealthy, comfortable group. They were well dressed, and both men and women had adornments that glistened in the bright light. Their faces were somber and unfriendly. Noah had the sudden realization that this could be the most difficult group he had spoken to in months.

And then the thoughts came, thoughts about his message, thoughts about making what he had to say softer and easier for the listeners to accept. He had become tired of the continual confrontation, the rejection, the ridicule, the abuse. He just wanted to have an easy night and go home, where he could be safe with Tess. He got an image of their reaction in his mind. He could see the frowns and hear the insults. He could see them getting up to leave. That was the hardest for him—speaking to the backs of people as they were walking out. For once, he just wanted to say a few words, make a few points, perhaps hear some agreement, and have somebody come afterward and say, "Now *that* was good preaching!"

". . . helped build the healing center for the deformed children, before we had light disintegration to eliminate the problem of those sad cases before birth. He also worked with the group that set standards of care for older people, again before light disintegration . . ."

I could leave out the part about sensuality, Noah thought to himself. He shifted in the chair. *Maybe I won't talk about the ship,* he thought. *I could just talk about the open violence, which almost everyone is against. That's it, I'll just talk about the open violence . . .*

". . . in summary that Noah Seth-Lamech used to be one of the most well-respected citizens of our region. Perhaps some of what you have heard about him is not true. In any case, I invited him here tonight to explain to you in his own words what he's doing. Please welcome him warmly."

As Noah stood, a remarkable thing occurred.

The people began to clap their hands.

Noah hadn't heard that sound in years. The last time was in a small God-house in a farm area. The speaker there was an old man who had been a spiritual father to Noah, and the listeners were all old men and women. They had listened to him carefully and voiced their approval openly. A strong sense of sadness surged through him as he remembered that most, if not all, of those people were now dead.

Noah shook the hand of the speaker and walked up to the speecht-able. The clapping was still going on, leaving Noah stunned. Everything in him wanted to tell this group what they wanted to hear, to finally be in the good favor of somebody.

And then the speaker's words came back to him, the words that spoke of the light disintegration of the deformed and old. *How can I tell pleasant things to a group that accepts that?* he thought. And then more words came into his mind, a few words that made him smile. They were Tess's last words to him before he left to come here: "No compromise."

No compromise.

Noah held up his hands and the clapping died down. "I thank my friend of five hundred years for his gracious comments about me. They're more than I deserve. In truth, all that I've done, God's done for me."

Noah felt his strength returning. He prayed for spiritual power. "This place where you're sitting is called a God-house. It's a place

where people are supposed to come together and talk about God. Tonight, that's what I'm going to do — talk to you about God.

"When I was a little boy, it was a much simpler time. You could
talk about God freely, and people — most people — knew what you were
talking about. Most people only had one husband or wife. Families
stayed together. Sexual immorality wasn't accepted. People weren't
killed because they were called 'useless' by some self-anointed leaders.

"But now it seems that the times are not so simple. Our lives are
lived at a pace that leaves us breathless. We don't seem to have time to
ask ourselves what we're doing to our lives and the lives of others. We're
running too fast to notice the more important things of life — things like
why we're here and what the best ways are to spend our lives.

"As a young man, I was the same way. I was running fast, but in
the wrong direction. Then one day, in a little God-house in an area far
away from any big cities, God touched my heart and showed me a
better way."

He noticed a few people shifting in their bodyrests. He asked God to
make him stronger, even more effective. "God showed me two things.
First, He showed me that He loved me, that He wanted me to belong to
Him. That was important, and goes along with the words 'God Is Love'
that you have over your entryway. God *is* truly love.

"But He showed me something else, too, something just as important.
He showed me that He's a holy God who hated my *sin* as much as He
loved *me*. He loved me so much that He wanted me to be in His family,
but I couldn't go in because my sin stood in the way. I knew the Code of
Adam as well as anyone, but I hadn't obeyed it. My sin had condemned
me to the pit with no way to experience and bathe in God's love."

Two people near the back got up and left the room. Noah prayed for
them quickly and then picked up his pace. "But God's love found a
better way. He knew I was too weak to obey the Code, that I was a
Code-breaker with no hope of being anything else without Him.

"And that's what I learned in that little God-house — that God had
provided a way. The speaker shared the beautiful words from the early
part of the Code, when God is speaking to the serpent, cursing the serpent, and then makes the promise: 'I will put rancor between you and

the woman, and between your seed and hers; he will tread your head underfoot, and you will bruise his heel.'"

Several more people left. Noah also prayed quickly for them.

"Even before the speaker explained it, I knew for the first time what those words meant. I had sinned like Adam; I deserved to die like Adam; and I deserved to go to the pit forever, like Adam. Like Adam, I couldn't obey the Code; like Adam, I could be easily led astray; and like Adam, I couldn't be good enough to earn God's favor.

"But God in His graciousness had provided a way—*the* way. He would send a serpent-slayer, a death-destroyer, a child descended from Mother Eve—but a holy child who would be our *Redeemer*. This Redeemer would be bruised—*killed*—by the serpent, and the shedding of His holy blood would satisfy God's demands for justice. He showed this in symbolic form by slaying animals and clothing our ancestors with the animals' skin. This painting over here shows that very time."

The stream of people departing was increasing, and Noah could hear the familiar grumbling. He prayed again for wisdom. "Why does sacrificial death make us so uncomfortable?" he asked, tears coming into his eyes. "Why is it so hard to believe that sin demands judgment, and judgment demands death? Someone *does* have to die for sin. But the question is: Who will die? You, for your sin? Or someone else, a holy someone else, who will die for you?

"And that's God's way. You accept this coming Redeemer by faith as *your* Redeemer, or you reject His offer and die for your sin. Why will you die? Why will you die, when you can live?"

"Why don't *you* die?" a man shouted from the left side. Many grunted in approval.

Noah smiled. "I *will* die," he said softly. "Or more accurately, my *body* will die. But once you've let faith guide you to this coming Redeemer, you know this world isn't your home. You know that when your body dies, He'll take your spirit home to be with Him."

Several people laughed. A tall man near the back came down the aisle and pointed at Noah. "Be quiet!" the man commanded. "We don't want to hear any more of this foolishness."

Noah stared at him. "Friend, it used to seem like foolishness to me, too. But it isn't. It's the way to life."

"I said 'be quiet!'" the man shouted.

"I *won't* be quiet," Noah responded with power. "You're going to leave this life, but you won't escape. Nobody stays dead. Some will live to be with God, and others will live to be with the serpent."

"Then why are you building that ship?" a woman to his right screamed. "Why don't you just die in the disaster you predict, and go to be with your God?"

"Because," Noah said, looking at her, "God's new life isn't just for *after* your body dies. It's for this life, too. Accept His Redeemer by faith. If you do, you'll have life forever with God, you'll have the power to finally and fully obey the Code that no one can follow without God, and you'll have the wisdom to get on that 'foolish' ship and live for Him for a while longer on the earth."

His defense of the ship was too much for the crowd. Many stood up and began screaming at Noah. One man shouted to the speaker sitting behind Noah, "Make him stop talking! We hate him!" The crowd picked up the chant. "We hate him! We hate him!" Noah felt something sharp strike his face. He put a cloth over the wound but stood unmoved.

Noah felt the speaker tug at his arm. "Sit down, Noah. They can't hear you anymore. You might as well sit down."

But Noah would not—could not—sit down. He walked around the speechtable, stood nearer the crowd, asked God for power, and pointed at the people with an intensity that he knew was not his.

"Who do you think you are?" he demanded. The people quieted down almost immediately. "Just who do you think you are? By your words and actions, you prove what I've been saying! You're so full of violence that it comes out of your mouths without restraint. And make no mistake: it's the *violence* of this age that's pushed God too far. He hates all of the rest—the immorality and greed and mocking of His laws—but it's the violence that's set His heart on destroying all this world that you're clinging to."

He was amazed that they were listening quietly. He felt the words and power pouring through him. "Do you think God's going to allow us to kill unborn babies, and deformed and sick and unwanted children, and old people called 'useless,' and still let us live and enjoy this earth? No!

Never! Give it up! Accept Him by faith and become people of peace!"
At this the people once again went wild.

"Please sit down, Noah," the speaker begged in his ear. Noah looked
at the hatred on their faces. He shook his head, took several steps back-
ward, and sat down.

"I'm sorry," he could hear his old friend saying. "Somehow, I
thought if we gave him a warm greeting he'd restrain his comments.
Obviously I was wrong." He held up his hands. "Please sit down," he
said in a pleading voice. Gradually the crowd quieted.

"Do you remember," he said to the disturbed group, "when I
preached to you about 'negative thinking?' Here tonight you've seen a
perfect example of it. Here's a man who used to be so positive, one
who thought about the possibilities of life. And now here he is, talking
about death and bloodshed and . . . and all kinds of terrible things. Why
isn't he happy? Because one night he had a bad dream and started
building a ship."

Noah wanted to say something, he wanted to run, but he felt numb
and sat motionless. "Noah Seth-Lamech," the speaker continued, "for-
gets that we are 'grace believers' and that our god is love. He speaks of
judgment and wrath, but he must be speaking about another god, because our god is love. I'm sorry I brought him here to bring negative
thoughts into our happy god-house."

He looked around at Noah and then back at the crowd. "Go home,
my friends. Next week, we'll talk again about positive things." As people finally began to leave, the speaker looked at Noah again, shook his
head, and walked out of the room.

Noah sat until everyone had gone. He took the cloth from his face
and saw that he had lost quite a bit of blood. He stood up to leave. As
he walked down from the speaking area, the old painting caught his eye.

He walked over and stood in front of it, just a cubit away. He was
startled to read the description at the bottom: Painted by Bethua Seth-
Enosh in the year 245 A.C. — painted while Adam and Eve were still alive.

His eyes scanned the image and saw that the man in the shining
robe was crying, just like Adam and Eve. His face looked so real that
Noah felt he could reach out his hand and the eyes would turn to look at
him. The face burned into his mind.

Noah's eyes finally came to rest on the feet of the man in the shining robe. Noah was overwhelmed by the sight, and thanked God for the confirmation of the truth that he had shared with these people just minutes before.

For there, almost lost in the fading colors, was the heel of a foot that had been bitten by a snake.

CHAPTER 8

P lease pass the bread," Tess said softly, below the din of conversation. She looked around the table at her family. On her left was Japheth and his spirited wife Sicilee. Sicilee had a heart-shaped face with high cheekbones and a slightly pointed chin. Her face was framed by light brown hair which covered both her forehead and her ears and was just long enough in the back to brush her shoulders. Her soft blue eyes always focused on whoever was speaking, and her joyful laugh could fill the room. She had become a real daughter to Noah and Tess.

Next to them was Ham and his new bride Nusheela, with her strikingly dark eyes. Ham and his wife appeared on the surface to be a perfect match. They were both dark-skinned and had broad faces. Nusheela's hair was black, tightly curled, and held in place in back with a jeweled clasp. She had a full mouth that seldom smiled.

On Tess's right was Shem, with his soft-spoken Melena. Shem had a wide mouth and was always smiling or laughing. He parted his hair down the middle and had it trimmed above his ears, all of which made him look very young. He had large brown eyes and a moderately long nose. Melena was a beautiful woman, with a narrow face, slender high-bridged nose, and a smile as rich as Noah's. Her long, dark brown hair draped down onto her shoulders. She had a boisterous laugh, which she seldom allowed to be heard.

Next to Melena was Noah's sister Naamah with her son Kenan. Methusaleh was sitting next to Noah. As Tess took the bread from Japheth she smiled at Noah, who was at the other end of the table and in an intense conversation with Ham.

"Ham," Noah was saying sharply, "I guess I'm just offended that you could give any respect at all to this rating system for people."

"I'm not saying I agree with the whole approach," Ham answered defensively. "I just think a lot of research has gone into these things, and I don't think all of those experts could be wrong."

"I agree with Dad," Japheth interjected as he leaned in front of Sicilee. "I've read some of that 'research.' I think they've already decided that some people are worth less than others, and they're just creating a fancy thoughtplan to try to make it legitimate."

"Exactly," said Noah, pointing at Japheth. "Exactly. Dividing people up into five 'kinds,' like they're animals. And then giving each 'kind' a different set of rights." He shook his head. "Only those of the first order get to participate in government. Only the first two orders have property rights. And only the first three get protection by the government."

"And then there's those poor 'fours' and 'fives,'" said Tess, shaking her head. "No rights at all. 'Fours' are slaves, just so much trash. And then there's the 'fives' . . ."

"But look at what they've learned from the use of the 'fives,'" Ham said in an excited tone. "You can't deny that their use in healing research has settled many tough health issues."

"I think it's disgusting," said Melena, breaking a long silence.

"I do too," added Shem. "To say that just because of your family background, you can be selected by the government for terrible healing experimentation . . ."

"But look at what they've learned about the bodycode," said Ham, warming to the argument. "They've actually been able to learn about the way we're built, about the internal logicbox that makes us who we are."

"I think they were doing just fine before they became murderers," responded Noah. "As early as 1150 they were far into those areas, before there even *were* any 'kind fives.'" He looked next to him. "Grandfather, do you remember those early discoveries?"

Methusaleh looked very unhappy. "I don't think I want to get into this at all."

"I don't know why everybody's so excited about this nonsense," Naamah interjected. "We can't change anything, anyway. These things were decided long ago." She looked intently at Noah. "And we're 'kind ones' anyway. Our family has always been 'kind ones.' It's just not our concern."

"I think it *is* our concern," said Shem, very gently. "Aunt Naamah, if we let this violence go on, it will eventually swallow us up. I've already been the victim of it, and it's increasing so fast it's scary."

Japheth sat up straight. "I agree. All people are created by God and come from our ancestor Adam. Everybody. There aren't any 'kind ones' and 'kind fives'; there's only those who follow God and those who don't."

"And," Shem added quickly, "it's up to us, the descendants of Seth who have always been 'kind ones,' to stand up for those who have no voice."

"It's the line of Cain that's brought this in," Sicilee said as she put her drink down. "Cain brought in murder and violence, and theft and greed. Even his name means 'a possession.' Adam and Eve brought in sin, but Cain brought in murder and violence."

"In Nod," Noah added sadly, "they don't even look for missing children anymore. There's so many, they've just given up. You have to hire your own rescue team."

"That just kills me," said Tess with great emotion. "Little children, stolen for who knows what, and the authorities don't even listen."

"If you had ever seen some of those children," Kenan, speaking for the first time, said harshly, "you wouldn't feel so bad. Some of them are worse than their parents. I think they ought to make the whole city of Nod a 'kind five' and put it out of its misery."

Naamah held up her hand and pointed at Noah. "Noah, isn't that the point of your ridiculous project out there? You're saying by building it that the world is totally evil and deserves to be destroyed. You're saying the whole world *is* a 'kind five.' So why bother talking about these problems? Why do you care, if God's going to destroy the earth anyway?"

Noah took a moment before he answered. "Dear Naamah, the world *is* totally evil. It's evil beyond comprehension. But as God's people, we still have to speak the truth and try to rescue some from their sinful life and horrible future. I'm not God. Who knows if some will still repent?"

"And if enough repented," said Tess hopefully, "maybe God would hold back His anger and spare our world."

"Tess," Noah said with affection, "you're an optimist. And so am I. I can't control how people will respond, but I *can* control my life and live out and speak the truth as it's been passed down from Adam. I *can* be faithful to God's message, and then each person has to decide what he'll do. I'm not responsible for their salvation — but if I don't speak, I'll have their blood on my hands."

"And what *is* this message 'passed down from Adam'?" Kenan asked in a strained voice.

"It's a message of forgiveness to those who will repent and confess their sins, by the work of the coming Redeemer, and put their hope in Him. I heard this message clearly in the private appointments I've had with our faithful ancestors — Enosh, Kenan, Mahalalel, and Jared, as well as my father Lamech. It was promised to Adam and Eve after God discovered them in their sin. I'm only sorry that I didn't get to ask Seth, and Adam himself, this same question."

"That would have been something," Shem said with awe.

"Well," Methusaleh said slowly, "I *did* get to speak directly with Adam and Seth. It was about my two hundreth year, when Adam was very old. Adam had so many children — thirty-three sons and twenty-three daughters, if my memory isn't failing me. He had many thousands of living descendants. And I'll tell you this: Although I agree with you about salvation, I don't think that Adam would have agreed about God judging the world and destroying it."

Everyone looked at Noah. Methusaleh, still a strong person at 968, could speak with such authority that his age and experience alone often ended arguments. And now he had raised a fundamental question that raced in various forms through the minds of everyone at the table: Would Adam have supported Noah in his prophetic warnings? Or would he condemn Noah as a self-centered fool?

Noah began to nod and then looked at Methusaleh. "Grandfather, I have something to show you that I just discovered last week in the great historical library in New Eden. It's an image of the great Adamic council of 930 — the very year that Adam died! No one had even checked it out for viewing in almost ninety years." Methusaleh leaned back in his bodyrest. Naamah and Kenan became very pale.

Noah touched several presspoints on the arm of his chair, and a screen came down from the ceiling behind him. He pushed back his chair so everyone could see and then touched another presspoint. A faded image appeared on the screen: "Great Council of 930."

"I can't believe it!" Japheth said with awe. "I didn't think there were any available images of that event."

"Nor did I," said Methusaleh, almost inaudibly.

They watched and listened as men began to move on a distant platform. They were all dressed in a similar way.

"They must all be from the same family line," surmised Tess. Noah looked back at her over his shoulder. "You're right, dear." he said. "I've already watched this several times. It's the same family line — and also the *only* family line! These are the living sons of Adam — I think there are twenty-four of them."

"Incredible!" Ham said in a whisper.

"Which one is Seth?" asked Japheth.

"He's the one right next to the center chair, on our left," Noah responded. "When he became a man and had a family, something changed in the world. That was when people really began to call on and proclaim the name of the Lord."

"I remember," Methusaleh said slowly.

Noah patted his arm. "Tell us," Noah encouraged. He quickly touched a presspoint and the image stopped.

Several minutes passed before Methusaleh spoke. "I do remember," he said. "Seth told us that the spiritual revival that came at the time his son Enosh was born . . . well, that was when the growth of systematic knowledge leaped forward. He said . . . that would always happen, that spiritual revival would always bring tremendous growth in every area of life."

"Many of our early, important discoveries go back to that time," Noah added. "Enosh wrote that there were five things that allowed civilization to become so advanced."

"What were they, Dad?" Japheth asked.

"Well, the first was spiritual revival. Enosh thought that would lead to the second, which was godly men trying to apply God's laws in every area of knowledge. Those were the main two."

"What were the other three?" Shem asked after a pause.

Noah leaned forward. "The other three relate to the length of life and relationship to Adam. Number three was exposure at one time to the godly knowledge of many living ancestors. Next was having long life to be able to accumulate and develop knowledge. And finally, closeness in time to the perfect creation and bodycode of Adam himself."

"What does that all mean?" Ham asked impatiently.

Japheth looked annoyed. "What it means, Ham, is that spiritual revival is more important to advanced civilizations than all of your Upper Schools put together."

"I think we'd better see the image," Tess said, anticipating a quarrel. As the image began moving again they could see that Seth was laughing as he talked with the man next to him.

"He looks strong," Tess said. "He looks much younger than his age."

The image began to move closer to the platform. As it did, they could hear the crowd at the long-ago event become very quiet. The focus moved to the left, as all of the men on the platform stood up and looked in that direction. Everyone around Noah's dinner table held their breath.

"I've never seen Adam," Melena said with awe, "except in pictures."

"Nor have I," agreed Nusheela.

On the viewlife, two young men came through a door at the far left. They turned and looked back. Suddenly, the man—the first man—was standing in the doorway.

His appearance was so surprising that no one around the table could say anything. Adam moved very quickly onto the platform and gently squeezed each shoulder as he walked toward his seat. He waved at those at the other end of the platform, and then he sat down. As he did, the image moved to a close-up of Adam's face.

His face was darker than most of those watching had expected. This darkness was emphasized by his wavy gray hair and his short, graying black beard. His eyes were very dark, almost black. His smile broadened as those at the council began clapping.

"He doesn't look much older than me!" Tess said with surprise.

"I see where you got your eyes, Nusheela," Melena said with a laugh.

"He was the first man," Noah said in a loud whisper. "He was created perfect, a man without flaw. Only the death that sin introduced— only the dying—had any affect on him at all."

"I hope I look that good when *I'm* 930!" Japheth said admiringly.

"You won't if you don't work less hours," Sicilee chided, only half-jokingly. Japheth smiled at her and shrugged his shoulders.

Then the man in the center of the platform stood up. Everyone—at the long-ago council and at Noah's table—became absolutely still.

"Thank you all for coming to this council," Adam said in a ringing, clear voice. He sounded like a young man of 250. "As you know, we have been having these councils, and the related festivals, every five years for more than four hundred years.

"Those of you here for the first time should know that the original purpose for these councils was to renew old family ties—not to conduct business, which has become such a part of these proceedings. I asked for the first council in the year 500, when I realized that even with appointments I couldn't spend time with all of my grandchildren, much less my great-grandchildren and great-great-grandchildren. I knew the problem would only get more difficult with time.

"So, on my son Seth's advice, I agreed to a council format. Here, the younger generations could come and listen to what I and the second generation might have of value to share. We would allow time for questions. I . . ." He stopped speaking and tried to clear his throat. They were surprised to see that he was crying.

"I can't tell you," he said with great emotion, "how thrilling it is to see all of you and to know that every one of you belongs in a beautiful and amazing way to me and to Eve. God has blessed us and our love more richly than we could have imagined—and certainly more than we deserved.

"But I am so sorry about what my sin has done. God has forgiven me, praise His holy name, but the consequences still go on." He stopped again, wiping his face with his hands. "I've never spoken to you before like I know I'm going to have to right now. I know my time is short, and now the time for warning has come.

"What a sorry heritage a father can pass on to his descendants! Sin, death—what a . . . heritage." He stopped speaking for almost a minute.

"As I have written in my journal, every person must face this heritage, this sin, and find refuge in the coming Redeemer. He will be the One who must pay the price that none of us can pay, and He'll have to pay it with His blood — as He showed me when He slaughtered animals and put their skins on Eve and me with His own hands. The One I walked with . . . He . . . Himself will have to come and die." He shook his head with great sadness.

"Believe in Him and live! He's real, very real. I myself have talked with Him and hugged Him and laughed with Him — and broken His heart. I'll never forget the . . . look on His face when He found me in my sin. I hope that none of you will see that look when you meet Him face-to-face.

"But now I must do more than talk of salvation by faith in the coming, dying Redeemer. I must tell you more — terrifying things that God has shown me. For even now, I see many resisting God and refusing His great salvation. I see many following the way of Cain, my little baby who . . ." Again, he stopped speaking for a long time. No one else made a sound.

"I see, more clearly than I want to, the result of sin. It's not just individual death; as it grows, it can mean the death of . . . everything. Even now, there are some who are denying creation itself." He laughed. "Isn't that something? I was *there*. The first thing I ever saw was the beautiful face of my heavenly Friend, as I opened my eyes and saw Him breathing into my mouth. I was never a baby, never a boy. I didn't deserve to be the first man — but I was.

"And this is what God has shown me, the father of you all, and . . . the father . . . of sin and death. This creation will face two judgments — times when God will completely destroy what is." There was turmoil in Adam's audience, as well as in Noah's dining room.

"Because of the fruits of sin, God will destroy the world twice — once by fire, and once by water. I don't know the timing of these things, but I know that they're as certain as the fact that I had no mother, and no father but God . . ."

"Enough!" shouted Naamah. "Enough!" Noah turned the image off.

"What is it?" Noah asked, startled.

"You brought that in here to make a fool of grandfather and me!" Naamah said in a rage. "You find an old image and think it confirms your actions. Grandfather was at that council. Adam was an old man, almost ready to die. Old, dying men can say many things. Just because he said it doesn't make it true."

"But Naamah . . ." Noah interjected.

"No. I won't listen to any more." She turned to her son. "Kenan, let's get out of here. This man brings shame on our family and now goes too far—bringing shame *into* our family." She looked at Methusaleh. "Will you come, too?" Methusaleh sat perfectly still, looking straight ahead. Finally, Naamah and Kenan walked out. The others heard the outside door as it slid back into place.

"Grandfather?" Noah asked softly. "You *were* there. What do you think? What do you remember?"

Methusaleh finally looked at him. "I don't know," he said through tears. "I don't know. But please continue the viewing."

And Noah and his family watched the image into the early morning hours.

CHAPTER 9

He reached around in the dark room, trying to find the sound. Although he was still only half awake, he was beginning to realize that the sound was not coming from the timekeep next to his bed. He was panicked by the feeling that he didn't know where he was.

Finally, he sat straight up. "What is it, sweetheart?" He heard Tess saying in a sleepy voice.

"It's the project alarm, I think," Noah said, trying to focus his eyes across the room.

"What does . . . is . . ." Tess, still drowsy, couldn't finish her thought.

"It *is* the project alarm!" Noah jumped out of bed and walked quickly through the dark room to the table where the alarm was flashing and making a low, buzzing sound. He reached over the table and turned on a light. He found the presspoint marked "Japheth."

"I'm already in my transport," he heard Japheth's voice saying clearly. "I'll be there in five minutes, Dad."

"Be careful!" Noah said in a loud whisper. "You don't know what might be out there."

"I will," Japheth agreed.

"What is it?" Tess asked as she got out of bed. "Was that Japheth?"

"Yes. We have an alarm from the project. He's already on the way."

Tess frowned. "What could it be at this time of night?" She saw the look on his face. "Noah?" Still he didn't answer. "Noah," she said, grabbing his arm, "will he be all right?"

He looked at her but didn't know what to say. He went to his dressing area and tried to calm himself as he put on his clothes.

"Noah," Tess said, trembling, "I'm scared."

"I am, too," he agreed soberly. "I've got to go. Pray for us."

Noah ran to the parking area and got into his transport. As the view-imager in front of him came on, he quickly entered the project as his destination. A route guide appeared as the transport moved past the sliding door and onto the pathway.

Noah called Japheth's transport. "Japheth?" he said. "Japheth?"

"I can hear you, Dad," the voice came back. "I'm just pulling through the gate into the work area to the north of the ship. I don't see anything. Maybe I'll get out and . . ."

Noah heard a crash. Japheth began screaming.

"Son, what is it?" Noah pleaded as he increased the pace of his transport to 30,000 cubits an hour.

"I . . . I don't . . ." The voice trailed off. "Dad! Dad! It's a huge man. I've never seen anything like him. He's out of his mind!"

Long-forgotten thoughts raced through Noah's mind. "Tell me what he looks like, son," he ordered frantically.

"He's so big!" The sound of another crash came through the receiver.

"Dad! He's trying to break through to . . . kill me. His eyes are so terrible and . . ."

Noah was frantic. "Japheth?" Suddenly, Noah knew the awful truth. "Japheth, what color are his eyes?"

"They're black . . . no, gray . . . Dad, they're . . . changing colors!"

Noah felt sick. He remembered the nighttime raids many years ago from these earthly monsters. That was why he had moved so far away from where they were living. And now, they had come to his new home.

"Japheth," he shouted. "Don't get out of your transport! That's a Nephilim!"

Noah reached forward and touched another presspoint "Yes?" a surly voice asked.

"Is this Commander Station 45?" Noah asked.

"It is. What do you want?"

"This is Noah Seth-Lamech. Did you receive the alarm from project site 102?"

"We did," the man said matter-of-factly.

"Do you have commanders responding?"

The man at the other end laughed. "No."

"Why not?" Noah asked in disbelief.

"Because," the voice answered with disdain, "project site 102 is a nonresponse zone."

"What?" Noah was furious. "What are you talking about, man?"

"Your project is a nonresponse zone. That means we don't answer your alarms."

Noah fought to control his anger. "I don't have time to deal with that right now" he said, frustration filling his voice. "My son is being attacked . . . by a *Nephilim*."

"A what?"

"A Nephilim—monsters from the east. Surely you've heard of them! They're the sons of demon-possessed men and their chosen women. If they've moved into this area, we're *all* in trouble. You need to get some commanders out there—*now!*"

"I don't know what you're talking about. You're a nonresponse project. No exceptions. I think you're out of your mind. I'm clearing this line." The man ended the communication.

Noah angrily returned to his contact with Japheth but couldn't get an answer. As he sped into the work area, he realized that all of the area lighting was off. He had never seen the project site so dark.

He had almost put the Nephilim out of his memory. Now he remembered what terrible things these fallen ones had done in other places. Some had seized power and become insatiable tyrants, ruling without mercy over their helpless subjects. Some of these ruthless men killed their own people, and a few of them even devoured their victims' remains.

One of the Nephilim family lines, however, had gone completely out of control. Even bigger than their relatives, these deranged Nephilim attacked anyone in their way and brutally tortured their victims. They were violence incarnate.

And now they were here.

He moved his transport slowly through the area. Finally, he saw the back of Japheth's blue transport. He drove up quickly and stopped.

He slowly got out and walked around Japheth's badly damaged transport. All of the glass had been broken. He shuddered as he saw blood on the bodyrest where Japheth had been sitting.

He turned on his quicklamp and began to scan the area near the ship. As he got close to the ship, he saw what he had been dreading since he first heard Japheth scream. Feeling sick and weak, Noah was immobilized by the horrible sight.

Japheth was hanging upside-down by one foot from the side of the ship. A metal rod had been bent and driven around his ankle and into the ship. As Noah drew closer, he could see that Japheth's face had been beaten almost beyond recognition. His bodysuit had been ripped completely away. His body was covered with claw marks, all of which were bleeding at a frightening rate.

"My God," Noah murmured. "Please help me now." He began to run toward Japheth. "Dear God, please don't let my son be dead."

*   *   *

Noah watched Tess come into the narrow walkway of the healing center. She looked like a lost little girl.

"Tess, honey," he said as he walked up and hugged her.

"Is he . . . ?"

He had never seen her like this. "No," he said softly, "he isn't dead."

"Thank God," she responded weakly.

He helped her into a nearby chair and sat down next to her, putting his hand on her leg. "Tess, it is bad. It was a . . . a Nephilim."

"A Nephilim!" she exclaimed as she sat up. "A Nephilim! What are they doing here?"

"They go wherever sin goes. This region has been full of sin for many years."

"What did they . . . do to him?" she asked as she leaned back. She looked as though she would faint at any moment.

He paused before answering.

"They hurt him badly," he answered honestly. "The doctors won't know the extent of the damage until they get their reports in the morning."

"That's it!" she said, surprising Noah with her sharp tone. "That's it! We can't go on. If *they're* here we'll never be safe, not even if we hire guards to protect each one of us." She looked into his eyes. "You have to give up that project. They'll never let us alone. It's not worth our son's life."

"If I give up that project, Tess, it *will* cost our son's life."

She looked at him angrily. "I don't care about that project," she said coldly. "I only care about my son."

He tried to take her hand, but she pulled away. "Tess," he said, "if you care about your son, you have to care about that project. It's the only way out of this world and into the next."

"I don't care about that project," she repeated. "Not if it costs me my son."

He stood up, frustrated, and walked several steps away. All of the old doubts came back to him again. Was he out of his mind? Was he ruining his family? He asked God to help him, but the war of thoughts went on. He had always known this kind of thing could happen, but now that it had . . .

"Seth-Lamech?" a voice nearby asked.

"Who?"

"Are you Noah Seth-Lamech?" the young woman next to him asked again.

"Yes."

"This message came for you." She handed it to him and went off. He looked away quickly as he realized how indecent her bodysuit was.

"Fool," the note opened. "How do you like my new monsters? It cost me a great deal to bring them here, but I thought you would appreciate my effort. Nephilim for Noah. What a pleasant thought." Noah looked at the signature, crumpled the message, and walked toward Tess.

Mizraim had brought them here. The man's hatred was overwhelming. Suddenly Noah remembered Mizraim's size and huge hands, and the thought came to him that Mizraim himself might be one of the tyrannical Nephilim. Waves of terror swept over Noah.

"I fear him, God," he prayed. "And I fear the Nephilim. But I fear You more."

Before he got to Tess, he stopped and looked up. "Help me not to fear my enemies," he prayed in a whisper.

CHAPTER 10

W e believe the time has come to end this waste of valuable community resources," the dayreport concluded. "This obscene work is no longer funny or worthy of discussion. It is a drain that has already cost us over two thousand jobs, as the owner of a once-powerful empire uses his resources to build a project that insults all of us by its very existence.

"Therefore, we call upon all ruling bodies to do everything in their power to bring this work to a halt, commit the owner to a mind treatment center, and give his resources to the community distribution officer."

Noah put the dayreport down and looked through the window. With the power of the organization that issued it, he knew he would probably get his first visit before the day was over.

"Have you finished the dayreport yet?" Tess's voice came softly from the doorway.

"Not yet," Noah replied with a smile. He looked back down at the writing that had attacked him so viciously. "Actually, I think I *am* finished with it. Or maybe I should say, it's finished with me."

Tess came over and quickly read the report. "Mind treatment center, indeed!" she stammered, her face flaring in anger. "They don't even know you! They didn't even come out to talk with you."

"Facts don't seem to be a necessary ingredient of what's written anymore," Noah responded.

"Well, I'd like to give them a few facts!"

Noah was always surprised and a little amused when his soft and gentle wife became outraged and outspoken. "I don't think they're ready for you, tiger!" he said with a wink.

She looked down at him and tried to continue to look angry, but she laughed as she looked into his eyes. "You!" she said through her laughter. "How can I carry on a good grudge with you around?"

"It's no use, Tess," he said as he took her hand and pulled her down next to him on the bodyrest. "If we spent all of our time being angry and frustrated about all the terrible things people are saying about us, where would the joy be? Didn't Enoch say that we should always be joyful?"

"But how can we be joyful when there's so much hate?" Tess asked, sounding confused.

Noah patted her leg. "Because we've got God, and that's enough. They don't have God, so they don't have anything. We can preach to those who might listen and pray against those who lead others into sin, but mostly we need to rejoice in our great God, love and obey Him, and leave the judgment with Him."

"Sometimes I think He's too patient with these people."

"I know what you mean," Noah agreed. "Enoch also said that God is slow to get angry and rich in mercy and forgiveness. But Tess, aren't you glad? What if He'd taken *your* life before you accepted His coming serpent-slayer?"

Tess was quiet for a moment. "You're right, of course. I don't feel like agreeing with you, but I know you're right." She looked at him with appreciation. "I guess I'll let God be God."

"Good decision!" Noah laughed. "He really does a very good job of it."

"Do you know—" Tess was interrupted by the sound of a knock from the front door. "Excuse me," she said to Noah as she walked to a receiver next to the door in Noah's office. She touched a presspoint and asked "Who is it?"

"Quota officer," a voice from below answered.

Tess looked at Noah. "What do you want?" she asked the man.

"I'm here to see Noah Seth-Lamech. I have some things to review with him."

Noah sagged in the bodyrest. Finally he looked at Tess and nodded.

"He'll be right down," Tess said.

As soon as Noah opened the door he knew he was in trouble. The man, wearing the adornments of a man-lover, was glaring at him.

"Yes?" Noah asked, without inviting him in.

"I'm the area quota officer," the man said arrogantly. "I'm here to get a count of the number of man-lovers and other protected groups that you have working on your—your *project*," he said with disdain.

"I don't have any man-lovers working for me," Noah said quietly, "at least, as far as I know."

"What?" the man asked in disbelief.

"You heard me," Noah said as he stepped forward through the doorway. "First of all, I wouldn't keep a record of things like that. All it does is make those in the 'protected' groups think they should get something for nothing, and hateful when they don't get it. And those in the other groups think they're getting nothing for something, and hateful to have to give it. It makes hatred *greater,* not less."

The man stepped toward Noah and stared into his eyes. "Who do you think you are? Don't you know that this is the *law?*"

"Yes," Noah spoke slowly. "Yes, I know it's the law. But it's a terrible law. It contradicts everything we know about God's law and justice. I won't obey a law that stands against God."

"You *have* to obey it," the man sneered. "It's the law, and you *have* to obey it. You have to keep a record, and you have to hire man-lovers and woman-lovers and child-lovers and . . ."

"Be quiet!" Noah thundered. "Be quiet!" The man backed up several steps. "All I *have* to do is obey God. I'll obey man's law when it follows God's law. When it doesn't, I'll disobey man's law. Men being perverted with men, and women with women, and men and women with children, does *not* line up with God's law. He hates it. So do I. I won't hire that kind of people, and I won't count them, either."

"I don't understand . . ." the man said weakly.

"That's right," Noah agreed. "You don't understand. If you did, you'd give up your sin and ask to be counted as one of God's own."

At this, the man began to move away. "You won't get away with this," he shouted over his shoulder. "I'll have the regional authorities begin proceedings under Regional Dominion laws. The government will end up owning your property!"

"This government," said Noah, "will end up owning nothing but a watery grave."

As the man went through the front gate he bumped into Shem, who was hurrying into the greenspace.

"Excuse me," Shem said quickly.

"We'll own you," the man hissed at Shem and then ran quickly away.

"What was all that about?" Shem asked Noah.

"That was our regional quota officer," Noah announced. "He's quite an interesting person."

"Hmmm." Shem watched the man getting into his transport. "I don't know how interesting he is, but I don't think I want him to own me!"

Noah nodded in agreement. "I can see why. That man is so full of sin that he spends his life trying to get other people to accept it — even *elevate* it."

"What does he think of our project?"

"Well," said Noah, "he thinks we're the most disgusting thing in the region. We won't deliberately hire people like him, and we won't track quotas, and we don't intend to, either." Noah eyed Shem closely. "He threatened to get us with Regional Dominion."

"How does that work?"

"Well, they take your land and they give you some money. They decide how much money."

Shem looked troubled. "Can they get this done before — "

"No," Noah shook his head. "No. I'd be very concerned, but it'll probably take them a year to get it through their system. In six months, it won't matter to them anymore."

"It may not matter to *us* if we don't get the box finished," Shem said sharply.

"I gather it's not going well?"

"No. Not at all. There's been a tremendous decline since Japheth was hurt. He really kept things going."

"What do you suggest?"

"Meta has a new supervisor he'd like to hire to help him," Shem answered. "I talked with her. She's a very lovely woman. She even talks about God."

"Really?" Noah asked with interest.

"Yes. Maybe she'll be one we snatch from the coming wrath."

Noah thought with excitement about the possibility of someone joining his family at last. "What's her name?"

"Dainea," Shem offered. "Her name is Dainea."

"Dainea," Noah said softly. "Let's pray for her, Shem."

Noah and Shem stood in the greenspace, praying for Dainea, until Tess called them for midday meal.

CHAPTER 11

People streamed past him along the busy second-floor walkway. He looked through the tinted glass encasement at the mammoth structures across the pathway and marveled at the newest one under construction—a cylindrical tower with gray reflective glass that would be almost two-hundred stories high when it was completed.

Noah smiled wryly as he reminded himself that this building would never be completed. The workmen were so busy, and it was all for nothing. He had tried to talk with them about God, but they wouldn't listen—they were sure that everything would continue as it always had, and wanted to carry on business as usual. When he had tried to talk to them at a lunch break, they had laughed at him. As he had walked away, one of them had thrown a lunch container at him.

The elemental-powered transports choked the main pathway below. He laughed to himself as he thought about transports that were able to go safely at incredible speeds being reduced to a rate that a crawling baby could pass. He watched as a man got out of one transport, walked to the one stopped in front of him, and began to hit the driver through the window.

"Dear God," he prayed quietly, "how long can You put up with this?"

People cursed each other as they passed. Any inconvenience, any interference, would bring on a tremendous outpouring of anger. People who were dressed in exquisite clothes were pushing and shoving each other. Each person acted as though he was the center of everything.

One man just ahead of Noah made a threat to an obese person whom he couldn't get around. When the man made no effort to move, the other man carried out his threat and hit him hard in the lower back. The overweight man slumped to one knee.

A commander pushed past Noah and several others and grabbed the attacker. "What's the matter with you, you fool?" the commander shouted. Noah saw the man turn around. He had a horrified look on his face. "Please don't hit me," he pleaded.

The commander began to club the man with a short stick. The man began to scream. That only made the commander angrier, and he beat the man even more severely.

Noah closed his eyes and prayed. The authorities had become brutal thugs, just like the people they were supposed to control. Noah wanted to intervene, but he knew the penalty for interfering with a commander — instant death at the commander's hands.

Stories of abuse were widespread. Many cases were settled by commanders on the spot and never made it to the courts. Most people hated the authority that these commanders wielded; but they were afraid to protest and afraid of what the city would be like if the commanders were held back.

Finally the commander pulled the man off the walkway at one of the store entrances, and Noah was able to escape the horror and go outside.

The view down to the end of the pathway was breathtaking — huge buildings of every possible design and material; an overhead transport system that moved swiftly and silently; airships landing and taking off from buildings. It seemed so real, so permanent, that Noah found himself wondering whether it would really all be destroyed. And then he knew in his heart that these things were like a dream that would be gone and forgotten when God awakened His full wrath and swept them away. He was struck by the thought that his funny wooden ship had more value than all of this man-made beauty, and would last much longer.

As he began to walk along the first-level walkway, he glanced at a store window on his right. He looked away instantly, shocked at the full-sized sign depicting sensual abuse with animals. He found himself unable to shake the image from his mind. "How stupid," he said, frustrated with his carelessness. He walked on with his head cocked toward the street to avoid any further images.

"Hey, you," he heard someone say to his right. "Look at this."

He felt the man pushing a piece of paper into his hand. Noah looked down to see an offering—all he had to do was go up two stories and women were there for any purpose that a degenerate man could imagine. The paper was full of obscene pictures.

"Why are you doing this?" Noah asked.

"What?" the man answered. "Why am I doing what?"

Noah shook his head. "Why are you making people sin? Why are you helping them ruin their lives?"

"Look," the man said, "I don't know what your problem is. All I want to know is, do you want to accept this offer or not?"

Noah stared at him. "I'll make you an offer instead," he said, trying to keep himself under control. "You can get out of this terrible life—if you can call it 'life.' You can find spiritual peace. You can escape from the wrath that's about to come on this sin-ridden city. And you can do this without paying me anything. All you have to do is give your life to God."

The man stared at him in disbelief. "What are you talking about, you . . ."

"Careful," Noah warned. "I don't have to listen to your filthy language. I *won't* listen to your filthy language! The time's too short. Either give your life to God, or take your miserable business elsewhere."

The man started to curse but stopped as Noah's gaze rested on him. "Just give me back my paper," he finally said in a whining voice.

Noah crumpled the paper in his hand. "You won't use this one to snare another victim." Noah stared at the man until he turned and walked swiftly into the building.

Noah arrived at the consumables store and went in.

"So it's you again," the man behind the counter greeted in a friendly voice.

"Yes, it's me. Do you have time to check some calculations on your logicbox before I give you an order?"

The man nodded and took the information from Noah's hand. "More grain?" the man asked, grinning. "You bought enough to fill up a tenth of your ship last month! What are you going to do, take herds of animals with you on your journey?" The man laughed as he went to the back room.

Yes, Noah thought to himself, *I am going to take animals with me.*
He didn't know how the details were going to work out, but he knew he
had to take enough grain to survive the journey—and then to feed every
living thing on his ship until crops could be grown on the changed earth.

The man returned after about five minutes. "It all checks out," he
said, handing Noah the results. "In the last six months, you've spent on
food what I earn in three years. I'll have it all out there in four days,
including the seed—although I don't know why you need to take seed
on a ship."

Noah smiled. "Elimel, have you thought any more about God since
our last conversation?"

"Well, some," Elimel answered uncomfortably. "But you know, I'm
so busy."

"Too busy to save your life?" Noah asked as he moved his arm
toward the hand-line reader.

"How much will it cost?" Elimel asked straightforwardly.

Noah was startled. "I . . . uh . . . I don't know what you mean."

Elimel leaned forward and put his arms on the counter. "I mean,
how much will it cost me to get on your ship?"

Noah smiled at the thought. "No charge, Elimel. There's no charge.
It's God's ship, not mine. All you have to do to get on that ship is
believe God and come. We'd be happy to have you. In fact, I think we'd
have to have a celebration if you came."

Elimel stood up. "I don't think I'm worth a celebration."

"But you *are,*" Noah insisted. "God rejoices when anyone repents
and comes to Him in faith. If God's people are really like Him, they'll
rejoice, too."

"Noah, you're not a bad man," Elimel said cautiously, "and I don't
think you're out of your mind, like everyone says you are. You've certainly given me a lot of business. But I don't think I want to talk any
more about God with you right now. Maybe another time."

Noah looked at him intently. "If you change your mind, Elimel, you
come talk to me—any hour of the day or night."

The man nodded. As Noah picked up his papers, he looked at the
receipt which showed he had made a cash transaction. He remembered
the early temptation to buy on credit, with the realization that he would

never have to pay many of his accounts. God had spoken to him strongly that the coming flood was no excuse for him to sacrifice his integrity.

After he had made this decision to avoid credit, he had laughed for a long time, as it dawned on him that extra money in the new world — with only his seven family members and perhaps a few others — wasn't going to be worth anything anyway. He had imagined trying to buy lunch from Tess with the then-useless money and hearing her say, "Noah!"

Noah turned and started to walk out. He suddenly realized that the store was unusually quiet. He thought it was strange that there was no one else in the store.

And then he saw him.

A Nephilim.

He had been hiding in a corner of the store, behind some cabinets. He now stood up. Noah was overwhelmed as he realized this monster was half again as big as he was.

"Storekeeper," the Nephilim said in a deep, resonating voice, "lock your door — now!"

"Yes, I . . . I . . . will," Elimel said in a voice full of terror. "I'm sorry, Noah," he said. He reached up behind him and pushed a press-point. Noah could hear the front door lock.

"Now go away!" the giant shouted at Elimel. Elimel was gone before Noah could look in his direction.

"Now, preacher-man," the demoniac said in an unearthly voice, "now we will see what you will do against us."

Noah saw that he had no way out through the front. He looked behind him to see if he could make it over the counter and out the back in time. He started praying for deliverance.

Before Noah could even finish praying, the giant lunged at him and swung his huge arm, hitting Noah in the side. Noah crashed against a table. The giant moved in closer and slapped Noah's face with his gnarled hand. Noah felt blood rushing from his eye and nose. The enemy roared at the sight of blood. Noah knew that the next blow could be the last one.

But he had faced these demon-possessed monsters before when he had once lived near their homeland. He had left to get away from them and their wild rampages, but not before he had learned their secret—and the way to defeat them. He began to pray again.

The Nephilim grabbed Noah by the neck and lifted him off the ground. Pain shot through Noah's head and back. "Now you will die, preacher-man," the living horror said. "We will snap your neck like a little twig."

Noah was looking his foe in the eyes. The terror was so real—the eyes were black and evil, the face huge and sickening, the teeth large and twisted. Noah felt himself giving away to an overwhelming fear. He couldn't even find the words to pray.

And then, suddenly, Noah felt a Presence and the fear somehow seemed less. He had forgotten for a moment who was on his side, but now, looking into the hideous face of this terrifying enemy, he remembered. Noah told himself that there was something—Someone—more real than ugly Nephilim, twisted men inhabited by unseen spirits. And he knew that it was time to do more than pray.

"In the name of the one true God," Noah said, gasping, "I command you to go."

The Nephilim's look changed. "Quiet," he shouted. "Don't say that name!"

"I *will* say it! In the name of God, go!"

Now the Nephilim was the one in terror. He dropped Noah and began to back away. "Who do you think you . . ." he roared.

"Go!" Noah, lying on the ground, commanded. "In the name of God and His coming serpent-slayer, go!"

The monster put his hands over his ears and screamed at the words. Noah pointed at him. "May my coming serpent-slayer cut you to pieces," he said, almost fainting. "In His name, go!"

The giant crashed through the front door.

Noah tried to get up, but his side hurt so much that he dropped back to the ground. He called for Elimel, but there was no answer. He began to pull himself across the floor. He got to the door and swept the safety glass away with his hand. With great pain he pulled himself through.

He called out for help, but no one would stop. He crawled back the way he had come, with people stepping around him and over him. Many cursed him. He stopped at one point to wipe his face with a cloth he carried in his pocket. He fought discouragement every moment of his long journey.

He finally arrived at his transport. As he pulled himself up, the sight that met him caused him to groan. His transport had been defaced — scratched with unspeakable blasphemies. He pulled himself into the front compartment and finally settled back into the bodyrest. He laid his head back and closed his eyes.

It's too much, the thought came. *It just isn't worth it.* He thought how easy it would be to quit, to stop the project, to just die in the flood and be with God.

"No!" he suddenly said out loud. He knew in his heart that wasn't the way. He knew these discouraging thoughts couldn't be from God. He told himself that with God's help, he would go on.

But when he opened his eyes, he realized that he was still in the middle of a nightmare.

There, written in blood on his control panel, he saw a message that chilled him and made him cry in frustration: MEET ME OR YOUR WIFE DIES.

CHAPTER 12

A s Noah went up the innerlift to the 150th level of the huge tower, he felt panic seize him. He had struggled all night and through the morning about whether he should come to this meeting.

Everything in him wanted to take Tess and his family and run from that region. He had thought how he might be able to build a ship somewhere else that would still satisfy God's requirements. He had even spent two hours making calculations about the resources he would need to accomplish such a feat in five months. He knew it was hopeless before he even sat down. In the middle of the night, he finally gave up and went to bed. He couldn't sleep because of the pain from the Nephilim's attack.

He and Tess had talked into the night about the attacks on Japheth and him. At Tess's urging, he had agreed to hire guards to protect her and the other six. He had refused to hire guards to guarantee his own safety. "We don't have enough money to hire that many guards,"he had told her. "Only God is powerful enough to protect me."

And now here he was, going up alone to the office of an evil man who had brought Nephilim into the region in his desire to crush Noah. Noah knew he had to stay and finish the ship of refuge, no matter what challenges he might face. He knew he couldn't run. He knew he had to trust God to protect him and his family in this time of great crisis.

Tess had reminded him of that in the darkness, before they had risen that morning. "Sweetheart," she had whispered into his ear, "do you remember what you said to me when we almost lost Ham through miscarriage? You said, 'no great challenges, no great faith; no great battles, no great victories.' Do you remember?"

And he had remembered, clearly. He had kissed her and thanked her for reminding him of what he had first told her. And so he had purposed not to run and not to hide, but rather to go and face his enemy.

The innerlift reached the 150th level and stopped. A mechanical voice intoned, "Thank you for visiting us—please watch your step." Noah looked up at the ceiling and said to the machine, "Even you don't sound very friendly." He walked off the innerlift and into the huge greeting room.

The splendor was overwhelming. Rich woods, carved and molded into exquisite designs, made up the walls. His feet sunk into the rich floor covering. A polished stone fireplace filled the corner to his right. He looked up to see the view-imager focused on him and following his moves. He smiled at it and waited.

Finally, a burly man came through a door at the far end of the room. "This way," he grunted.

Noah, limping, followed him into the majestic room; it made the greeting room pale in comparison. But the thing that caught Noah's eye was the view. He could see the entire region from this one room. He walked slowly over to one of the windows and stopped.

"You!" he could hear Mizraim command. "What are you doing over there?"

Noah looked in his direction. Mizraim was sitting behind a worktable with his hands on the table. Behind him stood the burly man who had led Noah in. Two other protectors sat in large bodyrests on the other side of the room. Noah looked back through the window.

"I'm just enjoying the beauty that you get to enjoy every day," Noah said without moving. "That is, *if* you enjoy it."

Noah looked back at Mizraim. "You do enjoy it, don't you, Mizraim?"

"I don't know what you're talking about," Mizraim growled. "I just want you to sit down."

Noah waited a moment before he finally went to the front of Mizraim's worktable and sat down. "You asked me to come," he said simply. "You left your invitation in my transport."

"Oh, yes," Mizraim said, grinning. "A nice thought, wasn't it?" He sat forward, glaring into Noah's eyes. "Actually, I never expected you to get back to your transport. From the bandages on your face and your limp, I'd say you almost didn't get back. How did you escape from that Nephilim?"

Noah grimaced, remembering the attack. "Let's just say that he ran into a power greater than his own."

Mizraim laughed. "Do you mean *you?*"

Noah shook his head. "No. Not at all. One more blow and he would have finished my life. But he never got to strike the blow. I called on the power of God, and that Nephilim ran like a frightened lake-swallower. In fact," he said reflectively, "he was about the size of a lake-swallower. But he was nothing compared to God."

"God!" Mizraim almost spit the word. "God! All I ever hear from you is 'God.' I'm sick to death about this false God of yours."

"Not false, Mizraim," Noah said calmly. "He's the one true God."

"Ha!" Mizraim exploded. "He didn't help your son Japheth, did He?"

"You admit you caused that?" Noah demanded. He stared at his enemy. "I knew it was you. Yes, Japheth is hurt much worse than I am. But he's alive, Mizraim. You can't kill someone when God is standing in front of him."

"I can kill anyone I choose," Mizraim said evenly. "I could give the word, and these three"—he waved his arm at the three protectors—"could kill you in less than a minute."

"Is this why you called me here—to show off your power and make threats?"

"No. I called you here to give you a last warning. Stop building that ship! I don't even care about your preaching anymore. Nobody's listening to you anyway. But that ship! It offends everyone. And you're paying wages that no one else can match. You're driving up all of our costs. It has to stop!"

Noah stood up. "And what if it doesn't?"

"If it doesn't," Mizraim said coldly, "then you can be sure that something much worse will happen to you and your family. *Much* worse."

Noah walked back to the window. He prayed for several minutes, asking God for strength. He waited quietly, and he could almost hear God saying to him, "Go, and I will protect you." Finally, he turned back toward Mizraim and his protectors. "I won't stop," he said in a hushed voice.

"What?" Mizraim asked. "What did you say?"

"I said I won't stop," Noah said more forcefully. "I'll never stop building that ship until it's done, and I'll never stop telling people why I'm building it until I get on it and the end—your end—comes. I *just won't stop.*"

Mizraim looked at him in disbelief. "You fool, don't you understand what I'm telling you? You *have* to stop. I won't allow you to continue. You don't have any choice!"

Noah walked toward the worktable. One of the protectors took it as a threat and moved toward Noah. "Sit down," Noah commanded him. The man looked at Mizraim, who nodded, and the man sat down.

"You don't have any choice," Mizraim repeated.

"You're wrong," Noah, standing over Mizraim, declared. "You're worse than wrong, but it'll be a while before you fully understand that. I *do* have a choice. And here's my choice: I'm going to continue. I won't stop, no matter what you or your friends do. You can count on it."

Mizraim stood up. "How can you not be afraid of what I can do to you?"

Noah shook his head. "You don't understand. I *am* afraid of you and what you can do to me and my family. But I'm more afraid of God and what He'll do to us if we don't obey Him. My fear of you is an unholy fear that will lead me to death. My fear of God is a holy fear that will lead me to life. If I've got to fear someone, then I choose God."

Mizraim was incredulous. "You've picked the wrong—"

"No, Mizraim," Noah interrupted, "*you've* picked the wrong thing. You chose your way and death. You can have it. I chose God's way and life." He turned and began to leave the room. "And I also choose to leave you."

"Stop!" Mizraim shouted.

But Noah never stopped. He walked into the greeting room, onto the innerlift, and out of the building. He never looked back once, not even as he closed the door of his home behind him, breathed a sigh of relief, and thanked his God.

CHAPTER 13

I've had it!" Ham said suddenly. Everyone stopped eating.

"What do you mean?" Noah, looking past Nusheela, asked.

"I mean I've *had* it," Ham said in a low voice. "I don't think I can stand the pressure anymore."

Shem, sitting next to Ham, turned to face him. "You've stood the pressure for years," he encouraged. "You can handle it."

"No, I can't," Ham insisted. "We're laughed at by everyone who knows us or even knows *about* us. I think it's time to stop. We've used up enough of our money anyway."

"I agree with my husband," Nusheela said in her deep voice. "We don't get invited anywhere anymore. I hate it."

"Life isn't made up of invitations," Japheth, sitting across from Ham and between Sicilee and Melena, admonished. His right eye was covered with heavy bandages. He was still badly bruised from the beating by the Nephilim and looked uncomfortable in his bodyrest. He had been allowed to leave the healing center for the day but was planning on returning for more care the next morning.

"I know how Nusheela feels," Melena lamented. "Being hated and ridiculed by everyone is a lot for anyone to bear."

"I know it's hard," Noah empathized. "It's *very* hard. But we have to hold on. I think we're less than five months from the . . . end."

"But how do you know?" Nusheela asked sharply. "How do you really *know?*"

"I know because I listen to the voice of God," Noah whispered.

89

"Dad," Ham said calmly, "we all know you're a good man, and you try to follow God's ways. We know that. But this whole thing is so . . . incredible. No matter how long we've been doing this, it never seems any less incredible to me. That ship is a constant reminder that I'm strange and different."

"You *are* different," Shem chided him.

"I don't need that kind of insult," Ham said angrily as he turned to face his brother.

"What kind would you like?" Shem asked innocently.

"Ham! Shem!" Tess commanded. "Please control yourselves at this table!"

"Sorry," Shem said, smiling at his mother.

Ham turned back toward his father. "Dad, Nusheela has a good question. How do you *know* all of these things? How can you think you're so right? How could so few of us be right?"

"How could so many of them be wrong?" Sicilee, sitting next to Noah, spoke for the first time. Noah moved his hand over to hers and squeezed it. He watched her face, intently but gently looking at Ham. He rejoiced in this intense young woman, who was fast becoming one in spirit with him.

"What?" Ham asked her.

Sicilee leaned forward. "Do you think the real question is 'how could so few of us be right?' Isn't the real question, 'how could so many of them be wrong?'"

"But *are* they all wrong?" Ham asked, staring at her.

Sicilee started to speak but changed her mind. "Go on," Shem encouraged her. "Answer the man."

"I agree," Tess added. "Sicilee, please share your thoughts."

"Well," she began slowly, "I certainly don't understand everything that's going on. But I know that this man" — she nodded toward Noah — "is different from others. He's a man of great fear of God and great faith in God. He's strong in his convictions but still gracious and gentle. I feel it's a privilege to share life with him. I know Melena agrees with me on these things."

In the pause that followed Sicilee's comments, Melena remembered how as a lonely, neglected, abused child, Noah had taken time to get to know her. She knew that he could have accepted her seemingly happy exterior as she sat with the other children around his greeting room for weekly studies of the Code. But with tenderness and intensity, Noah had learned over time of her painful life, and through prayer and wise counsel had helped her escape further loneliness and abuse.

At first, however, she had thought Noah was just another man who would take advantage of her. Yet it was through his devotion and pure affection that she had learned to trust Noah with her whole heart. This trust had led her to believe in a loving God who not only could protect her and provide for her, but who *would* do these things because He loved her.

"I also agree with those things," Ham said breaking the pause. "But what's that got to do with whether we're right about building this ship and making ourselves the trash of society?"

"I love my father-in-law too," Nusheela agreed. "But love doesn't always mean you think the person is right."

Sicilee shook her head. "I didn't say it was because of love alone that I would follow this man. I love him very much, but I follow him because he's a man who trusts in God and obeys everything that God tells him to do."

"I think we're just being proud," Nusheela said disrespectfully. "I think we have a real lack of love for people. Some people aren't so bad. They can't all be wrong."

"But what if they are?" Sicilee persisted. "What if they *are* all evil in the eyes of God? You see, I think that's the most amazing thing. I think they *are* all evil and that just overwhelms me. They're wrong, but how could so many of them be wrong? How can so many people reject God and His good way?"

"That's the way I have to think when I start getting discouraged," Tess agreed. "It's so hard to believe that millions and millions of people could be heading for total destruction. But then I look at what they do and how they speak, and it reaffirms that God's judgments are right."

"But we're expecting God to kill *all of them?*" Ham asked incredulously. "*All* of them? Maybe they're wrong. Maybe we're going to see some sicknesses and wars. But the total destruction of *everything?* It's too much."

"It may be too much," Noah said softly, "but it's still true. I remember the torment I went through when God first spoke this into my heart. I didn't want to believe it either. But He convinced me of two things. The first was that Adam was right; there would be two judgments, by fire and by water. I fasted and prayed for many days to ask God which one this would be. He told me this one would be by water and that the fire would come later and destroy everything. He told me to build a ship." Noah leaned back and smiled. "Given the fact of a worldwide flood, a ship made a lot of sense to me."

"I hope you're right, Dad," Japheth laughed, "because I don't think a wooden ship is going to do us a lot of good if this is the fire judgment."

"I don't think this is funny," Ham sneered as he stood up.

"Relax, brother," Shem said as he pulled on Ham's arm.

"I won't," Ham said, pulling away. "We're basing everything in our lives on Dad being right on every detail. I haven't gotten any vision about this thing, and neither have any of you. Doesn't that bother you?"

Japheth pointed at Ham. "What bothers me is you. Do you think that God only speaks to people directly? Don't you think that He might also speak to you through godly people in your life?"

"Please sit down," Tess said to Ham. He grudgingly complied. "I want to say something here," she said firmly. She took the time to look at each person around the table. "God has never spoken to me directly about this thing. Never. But part of love, part of faith, is following one you trust who is following the Lord." She looked straight at Noah. She smiled. "And I'll tell you this: Even if I have doubts about that ship ever being in water, I'm going to get on it. And I'm going to stay on it, until your father says it's time to get off."

"I feel the same way," Sicilee agreed. "I'm going to get on that ship at the appointed time."

"Well," Noah said slowly, "I really appreciate those commitments. But let me tell you something more." He watched as everyone looked at him, some with anticipation, some with dread. "It's the main thing I wanted to tell you tonight. After the discussion we've just had, I'd really like to wait, but I think it's important that you know things as I know things."

There was a long silence. Finally, Shem spoke. "Dad, you can tell us." He nudged Ham with his arm. "Even Ham wants to know."

"What next," Ham said rather than asked.

Noah pushed his chair back and crossed his legs. "I think it's possible that very few people will join us. That ship may have very few people in it."

Japheth looked startled. "Dad, if that's so, why would God have us make it so big? We know God can see into the future. Why would He have us waste so much effort?"

"I didn't say we wasted our efforts," Noah said. "I just said there may not be many *people* on that ship."

Shem leaned forward. "What *do* you mean, Dad?"

"I mean," Noah said cautiously, "that this ship is going to be full of living things. They're just not going to be people."

"What?" Japheth and Shem asked almost together.

"Think about it," Noah suggested. "If we really believe that God's going to destroy all people with a flood, then what about the animals? Everything that breathes is going to die, because for a long time there's going to be no dry land to stand on."

"So what are you *saying?*" Nusheela asked suspiciously.

"I see what he's saying," Ham, looking down at the table, said quietly. "He's saying we're going to a new level of ridicule. He's saying that we're going to take animals onto the box."

Japheth looked from Ham to Noah. "Dad?"

Noah nodded in agreement. "He's right. God made a complete creation. Animals and plants were put here for man to care for and use wisely. We already decided that we needed to take all kinds of seed. But what about the animals? Can we just let them all perish from the face of the earth forever?"

Melena was incredulous. "Do you mean we have to get on that ship with all kinds of *animals?*"

"That's disgusting!" Nusheela said. "Some animals are just so . . . disgusting!"

"Building the box is bad enough," Ham, looking up, said with conviction. "But do we have to start telling people we're going to bring animals on there with us, too?"

Shem tapped Ham on the arm. "People are already impressed that we're going to bring you."

Ham jumped up. "I don't have to listen to this! We hear one fantastic idea after another, and now this brother—"

Ham was interrupted by a tremendous crash only about a cubit from Tess. Tess jumped out of her chair, and everyone scattered from the table. After a few minutes, Noah cautiously crawled to the window. "It's a huge rock," he whispered. "Somebody threw a rock through the window."

"They could have killed Mom," Japheth whispered back. "What kind of people could do that?"

Shem stood up and looked at Ham, who was leaning against a wall in a corner. "The kind," Shem said very slowly, "that Ham doesn't think are bad enough for judgment."

CHAPTER 14

"I love him dearly," Melena said as she passed Shem a bowl of fresh fruit. "I've loved him since I was a little girl, and he and Tess would include me with your family. When my mother set aside my father, I never saw him anymore, and my mother just got . . . too busy. I think of your parents as my parents, but I don't know about all of this. This new information about animals has really shaken the family."

"I know," Shem agreed as he sliced off a piece of an apple.

"What do you think will happen?" she asked, slicing a piece of melon.

"I just don't know," Shem said, confused. "We may have lost Ham and Nusheela last night. But I think Japheth and Sicilee are really committed." He caught her eyes. "And what about you?" he asked with a grin.

"I don't know," she answered matter-of-factly. "I know he's a good man, but this whole thing is turning into a nightmare. It's always sounded . . . strange, but it just keeps getting stranger and stranger."

"So what do you want to do?"

"I'd like to move," she answered sharply. "If you really want to know the truth, I'd like to move."

"What?"

"I just want to get away from the whole thing," she said, slicing a piece of bread. "I'd like to run away from everything, including that ship."

Shem looked dismayed.

"Are you saying you aren't with me?" he asked.

She got up and walked to the waterprep area. She looked through the beautiful plants that filled the shelved window and sighed. "I'm with

95

you. You know that. I just don't know if I can get on that ship when the time comes. I think I'd feel too silly."

Shem got up and walked up behind her. "Sweetheart," he whispered in her ear, "I'd feel silly leaving you behind."

She turned and kissed him. "I'll probably get on," she said grudgingly. "But I won't like it."

Shem laughed. "You're something. Did you know that?"

"I did," she said with a smile. "Will you let me know what it is when you figure it out?"

He kissed her again and then started toward the door. "I've got to go. What do you have planned for the day?"

"Sicilee and Nusheela are coming over."

"May God help us men," Shem prayed, looking up with a smile.

"Get out of here!" Melena laughed as she threw a cloth at him.

Melena finished cleaning the food preparation area just as she heard the door alarm.

"Hello, dear," Sicilee said as Melena opened the door.

"Hello," Melena responded. "Come in, friends."

Sicilee went to a large bodyrest in the far corner of the room. Nusheela followed her and sat down on a low bodyrest near Sicilee. Finally Melena joined them, forming a tight circle.

"What did you think about last night?" Nusheela asked. It was obvious to the others how she felt and that she wanted them to speak first.

"Shem and I were discussing it right before you came," Melena offered. "I have to admit, I told him I thought things had gotten out of hand!"

"Me, too!" Nusheela eagerly agreed. "I think it's time we get our husbands to rethink this whole thing."

"I don't think you're really including yourself in that comment. You mean you think it's time for us to get *our* husbands to rethink things," Sicilee corrected.

Nusheela appeared hurt by the comment. "I didn't mean anything. It's true that Ham's lost his interest in the . . . project, but I don't think he'll actually stop his involvement until his brothers change their minds."

"I don't know how these men can be so dependent upon each other's viewpoints when they disagree and argue so often," Melena said.

"It's because they have a common heritage," observed Sicilee. "They have the same father and the same heritage of faith. It keeps them working together even when they're not in agreement on all of the details."

"I hope my children will stick together like that," Melena shared.

Nusheela leaned forward. "Are you trying to tell us something?"

Melena looked confused but finally caught on. "No," she said, laughing, "I'm not pregnant. In fact, I don't really want to have children right now."

"Why not?" asked Sicilee.

"The times are just too bad. I just can't see trying to raise children in a disintegrating society like ours. I'd feel like I was doing them harm."

Sicilee frowned. "I can understand your feelings, Melena, but I can't agree with them. I think children are a blessing from God. And times have always been sinful. If people had waited until there was no evil before they had children, *we* wouldn't be here talking about it! In fact, if Noah and Tess had waited, we wouldn't have any husbands!"

Melena laughed. "I guess you're right. But I don't see how we can really do anything to make sure we raise strong children, when everything around them wants to tear them down."

Sicilee slipped out of her bodyrest and onto the floor. "We can!" she said with conviction. "We can pray. And we can work." She paused for a moment before continuing. "But mainly, we need to live godly lives ourselves, lives that are full and rich and deep and joyful and balanced. I've grown in my faith by watching and following Noah and Tess. Shem and you would be good examples for your children. I think we *can* raise children who'll change things for the better."

"Then why haven't *you* had any children?" Nusheela asked in a surly voice.

"Because we haven't been able to," Sicilee responded with great emotion. "We want children; we've even been praying for children. But so far, we haven't been able to have any." Tears streamed down her face. "Japheth thinks it may be because of the drugs I took early in our marriage to keep from having children."

Melena crossed the short distance to Sicilee, sat down next to her, and hugged her. "It's all right, dear. God will hear those prayers."

Sicilee wiped the tears from her face. "I can't understand it. Japheth says it could be that God wants the next generation born in the . . . in the new earth to come."

"So that means you're definitely going to continue with this project?" Nusheela asked, a sharpness in her voice.

"Yes," Sicilee responded strongly. "Yes, we are. We've committed our hearts to this path, and we're never going to turn back!"

Nusheela looked irritated. "And how about you, Melena?"

"I don't know. Right now, I don't want to go. I may never really want to go. But if Shem gets on that ship, I know I'm going to have to get on it, too."

"Why?" Nusheela asked.

"Because he's my husband. I'm under his authority, and if he's following God and takes that ship, I'll have to take it, too." She let go of Sicilee and sat cross-legged in front of Nusheela. "Nusheela, the other reason I'd have to get on is that I have no other close friends outside of this family of eight. You can't—or at least shouldn't—be totally close to somebody who doesn't love God, and there just *isn't* anybody else who loves God."

Sicilee nodded. "I agree."

Nusheela looked uncertain. "I don't understand you two. I guess I'm outnumbered. But the one I really don't understand is Noah. How can he be so sure?"

❧ ❧ ❧

"But what if I'm wrong?"

Tess looked at her discouraged husband as he asked the question. He had struggled through the night, unable to sleep, frustrated with the discussion at dinner the night before. "I thought you'd put that question to rest long ago, dear," she said, tenderly.

He tried to smile. "You know I've never stopped the project. But I've never stopped the questions, either."

She sat down next to him. "So where do these questions come from?"

"They come from life," he said in a tired voice. "They just come from life. You know in your heart that you're on the right path, and you move ahead. Then somebody says something, and all your confidence is gone. You tell yourself that you're only going to listen to the Lord and you're going to ignore the discouragement. But then along comes one of these lovely beings called 'people,' and he knocks you down to the ground."

"You're thinking about Ham?"

"Yes, and Nusheela. Sometimes, I wonder where I went wrong."

"You don't *know* you went wrong," she encouraged. "You were the one who first taught me that we have to take the long view, God's view. You said that we think in terms of days and weeks and months, and He thinks in terms of generations. I really believe that with God's help, Ham will come around. You've always told me that if we fear the Lord, He'll bless our efforts with our children. No matter what else, you've *always* feared the Lord."

"You know, I think one of the main reasons God gave you to me is so that you can remind me of the things that I know, but can't remember where I put them." They laughed together.

"And another thing," she said in a mock preaching tone. "Remember what you said about God being our 'backup'? If we forget to discipline our children, He still disciplines them; if we forget to bless our children—"

"—He still blesses them," Noah finished.

"See," she said, poking him in the side, "you *do* remember!"

"Tess, I also know this: I don't think anyone else is going to join us."

"You don't know that."

"No, I don't know that. But I sense it in my spirit. I can't fully understand it. A whole region full of people, and we're the only ones who are going to listen to God and be saved from His wrath. How can that be?"

"I think I have the answer," she said. "Let's go to the viewing room."

They went to the other room and sat together in an old bodyrest. Tess looked at Noah. "I know that some of your questions come from me," she said softly. "Maybe many of them do. I know I was terrible when Japheth was hurt. Please forgive me." He nodded and kissed her.

After a pause, Tess turned on the viewlife and turned to the channel reporting the information of the day.

The first report was lengthy, reporting on the rampant pollution that was threatening the underground springs and the vapor canopy. "If we don't restrain ourselves," the reporter was saying, "we could bring the ultimate disaster—the unleashing of the water in our vast canopy."

"Noah!" Tess exclaimed. "Did you hear that? Maybe some *will* finally listen."

Noah frowned.

"They won't, Tess. If people won't believe God, they won't believe this report. Even if they did, they'll feel strange for just a few minutes and then go about their business."

Other reports followed in devastating succession. One covered shortages of materials and their exploding prices. Several reviewed the day's stealings of people, molestations, and murders; Noah had to turn the viewlife off several times because of the images shown. A final, short report covered some "supposed" reports of giants on a rampage in a rural area.

"Mizraim brought them in to hurt us," Noah lamented. "And he's brought untold disaster to the region. There *are* no good reports."

Tess took the control from Noah and turned the viewlife off. "Do you see what I mean?" she asked softly. "That's my point. There *is* no good information. You'd think people would see this and take it as a sign."

Noah stood up.

"They won't, Tess. They won't take it as a sign. They think it'll all go on this way forever. They'll complain about the problems, but they're enjoying their sins too much to demand a change, in themselves or in society. In fact, the only time they *do* demand a change, it's in the society. It's never in themselves. They think they can change the 'out there' without changing the 'in here.'"

"So what are you telling me?" she asked.

"I guess I'm telling you that the questions that come in the night are wrong. God's wrath *is* coming. And the serpent would like to make me doubt that. But we've changed the 'in here'"—he touched his chest—"and we're going to finish that ship."

Tess stood and hugged him. "You sound like you remember what you know," she whispered in his ear.

He took her face in his hands. "I do remember, Tess. Thank you." He pulled her close and put his mouth close to her ear. "May I never forget again."

CHAPTER 15

N oah was startled by the sharpness of the knock on the door of the project office. "Come in," he said tentatively.

As the door opened, he could hear the intermingled, comforting sounds of construction coming from the project. A round-faced, husky man with whiskers surrounding his mouth entered the office quickly and the door closed behind him.

"Noah Seth-Lamech?" he asked gruffly.

"Yes."

The man looked at Noah and then around the room. He finally came toward Noah and sat on the edge of the worktable. He looked intently at Noah. "Some project you've got out there," he said, smiling.

"Many people seem to think so," Noah responded evenly.

"Well, I'd heard of it, of course, and seen it on the endday reports, but I think it's one of those things you have to see to really . . . uh, appreciate." His smile grew broader.

"I'm glad you find it interesting," Noah said. He was very uncomfortable with the man and wondered if he were another government official here to harass him.

The man stood up, looked around again, and then sat in the bodyrest in front of Noah's worktable. "Tell me when you last saw your son Shem."

Noah was deeply disturbed. "Why do you ask?" he inquired, standing up.

"I'll ask the questions here. When did you see him?"

"Yesterday, in the morning. He had some planning to do, so he was going home early." Noah could read nothing in the man's face. "Please tell me why you're asking. Has something happened to him?"

The man became very serious. "Seth-Lamech, I'm Senior Commander Nahajel Cain-Irad. We received a message this morning from a pack that claims to have stolen your son."

Noah felt sick. He leaned back in his bodyrest. "Please, tell me . . . what happened."

"This came to us this morning," the man said matter-of-factly as he handed a note to Noah.

Noah opened the note and let his eyes slowly focus on the overwhelming words. "Dad," it read, "I've been taken by a pack. I think they have incredible power. They're watching me write this, but I don't think they'll object if I say they're consumed with evil. Their leader is reading this and smiling. They want all of our money—*everything*. Dad, I don't know if they'll let me say this, but I'll say it—*don't do it*. If you do, it will stop the project and you'll all die. This way, only I'll die. I'm willing to do that, Dad. Don't give in. I love you. Tell Mom and Melena and the rest that I love them." Noah saw Shem's familiar signature at the bottom.

"I think you're out of your mind," the senior commander was saying, "but I'll say this: You have a brave son."

"What do you—" Noah began, but stopped as he saw Tess coming to the door. As usual, she was bringing midday meal for them to share.

"What about his guards?" Noah asked quickly.

"Dead," Cain-Irad answered without emotion. "You don't want to know the details."

Noah nodded. "Please," he said to the man, "let me tell her." The man shook his head in agreement.

Tess came in, smiling until she saw the visitor. Noah remembered how glad she had always been to see visitors early in their marriage. All of that had been replaced over the years by suspicion as the culture had fallen apart.

Noah got up and went to her. "Welcome, dear," he said as he hugged her. "This is Nahajel Cain-Irad. He's a senior commander."

"Hello," Tess offered weakly.

"Please sit down." Noah whispered in her ear. He sat next to her in the large bodyrest in front of the window. "Sweetheart, this man has brought some . . . very bad news. Hold my hand, and then read this." He lifted her face to look into his. "But hold my hand tight," he said softly.

He watched her face change to an expression of horror as she read the note and the words sank in. "No!" she exclaimed, stifling a scream. "Oh, no," she said, sitting up. After a moment, she stood up and faced the officer. "What are you going to do?" she demanded weakly.

"I'm afraid there's not much we *can* do," the man answered without concern. "There's so few of us and so many of them, we can't take the time to try to find every person that gets stolen."

Tess seemed close to fainting, but now her anger kept her on her feet. "I can't believe this!" she said as she grabbed the back of the bodyrest. "They've got my son, and you can't do *anything?* What's the matter with you? What kind of a man are you?" Noah had never seen her so angry.

"I don't have to listen to this," the man responded with frustration. "I came to give you this information, not to take your abuse." He looked past her at Noah. "I'll let you know if we learn anything," he said as he turned and walked out.

Noah walked up behind Tess and tried to hug her. "No," she said, pulling away. She turned to face him. "You've got to give them the money," she almost shouted. "I don't care if we have to give them everything! I don't care if it stops the project!" She looked out the window at the ship. "Look at the grief it's brought to us! Nothing but grief. You've got to give them the money, Noah. You've got to get him back."

"But dear, please—"

"Don't talk to me about it!" she interrupted. "I don't care about the project or money or anything. I just want my son back! I couldn't get on that thing without him anyway."

"Sweetheart, I—"

"No! Stop! I want Shem. I want . . . my son. I want my little boy." As she said this, streams of tears came from her eyes. She staggered to the nearest bodyrest. He had never heard her cry like this, a deep moaning and wailing that completely broke his heart.

He sat next to her and touched her arm gently. "He's my little boy," she sobbed. "Oh, Noah, I can still see him through the window of our old home." She looked up at him, her face full of tears and smudges. "I can see him swinging and laughing," she said pathetically. "Remember his beautiful little laugh? Remember how he ran with such joy and abandonment?" She wiped her face with her hands. "Please," she cried, "get my little boy back."

Before he could answer, the door opened and Ham came in. "Is it true?" he asked.

"You talked with the senior commander?" Noah asked in a whisper.

"Yes. He told me everything." He started pacing back and forth. "Well, that's just great! They've tried everything, and now this! Ridicule, humiliation, and now a dead brother!"

At this, Tess broke down completely. Noah stood up, quickly grabbed Ham by the arm, and rushed him out the door.

"Do you know what you just did?" Noah demanded as the door closed behind him.

"What *I* did?" Ham asked incredulously. "I didn't do anything. But it's true, isn't it? Isn't Shem dead?"

"No. No, he's *not* dead. They've taken him, but I feel—no, I *know*—he's still alive. We'll get him back."

"How?" Ham asked, half-mocking. "Stolen people never come back. They always end up dead. And I hope you're not expecting any help from that obnoxious senior commander."

Noah shook his head and leaned against the wall. "No, I'm not. I'm only expecting help from God."

Ham hit his fist on the wall.

"Dad, I can't take any more right now. I've supported you in this thing, but I'm tired. I'm tired of the abuse. And now look at what this has done—it's cost me my brother." He waited for a response, but Noah just leaned helplessly against the wall. "Dad, Shem was going to lead the material search team to Tep-Gsepdotdu. I need a break. I've got to get out of here. I want to lead that team."

Noah looked at the face of his rugged son. He thought of Tep-Gsepdotdu, the infamous "den of pleasures" in the region of Nod. He had never sent Ham to that area because of his concern about the rampant immorality and its affect on Ham. But he could see that Ham was adamant.

"Will Nusheela go with you?" Noah asked, too weak to argue.

"I hadn't thought about it," Ham answered, changing his expression. "Why?"

"I think you should take her. It's a terrible place, and I think she'd be an anchor for you."

Ham snorted. "You don't trust me, do you?"

"Son, I don't have time to argue with you. I have to get back in there to your mother. But let me tell you this. Men are men. We can all be caught off guard by filthy images or people. Any man who tells you that he can get involved with those things but not really be affected by them is either a liar, or a fool, or both. Those things will tear down our spirits. You've got to stay away from that—even the little things, the things on the edges. If you don't, they'll swallow you up."

"So what are you saying?"

"I'm saying this. I don't really want you to go. But if you'll take Nusheela, I guess you can go."

"Agreed," Ham responded quickly.

Noah stood up straight. "You can come back later for the need list." He put his hand on Ham's shoulder. "Please, son," he pleaded, "please be on your guard."

"I will," Ham said confidently as he turned and walked away.

"Sorry I said that in front of Mother," he said over his shoulder.

When Noah walked back into the office, he could see that Tess hadn't moved. Her fierce crying had softened to a quiet sobbing. He went to her and sat down.

"Are you going to give them the money?" she asked quietly as he sat down.

He didn't answer immediately. "Tess," he said, looking out of the window next to the bodyrest, "I can't give them the money. If I did, they'd only . . . hurt him anyway. And I can't stop the project. I'm too afraid of the power and wrath and righteous demands of our God. I respect Him and honor Him too much to disobey Him. I just can't stop that project. If I do, we'll all die."

"I want to die," she groaned, burying her face into a pillow.

He looked down at her. "I won't give them the money," he said with quiet determination, "and I won't stop the project. But I'll form a rescue team to find him, Tess. With God's help, we'll get him back."

He turned her over and looked into her eyes. He took her face into his hands and kissed her tear-stained cheek. "We'll find him, Tess," he said with conviction. "We'll get our little boy back. We'll get that little boy on the swing back." He brought her face close to his. "Do you believe me?" he asked, his emotions choking his voice.

Finally, her eyes searching his, she nodded in agreement. "I believe you," she whispered.

CHAPTER 16

Do you understand?" the large man said tersely.

Noah studied the face of Jalel, the man he had asked to lead the rescue of his son. The broad and aging face belonged to a man who had seen and done everything he had ever wanted to. He had deep set, black eyes and a moustache. Although he was smaller than Meta, he was menacing in his appearance.

"I understand," Noah finally responded.

"I'm not sure you do," the man said gruffly. "You think Mizraim is behind this, and I probably agree. But that doesn't matter now. The pack he's brought into this is not under his control. I've run into the Demon pack before. They did this to your son. And they did this to me."

He reached down and tore open the top of his bodysuit. Noah was sickened by the site of a huge scar that ran from Jalel's neck to the middle of his stomach. It was so large it looked more like a welt than a scar.

"You see that?" Jalel asked. "They had me on the ground, and one of them pulled out a lance and started cutting. He didn't do it quickly—he probably took five minutes to very slowly make the cut. The whole time he did it he was laughing and spitting on me."

Noah looked away.

"So what are you saying?" Noah asked, as he looked at the unusual images on Jalel's wall.

"I'm saying this," Jalel, obviously irritated, said. "I'm saying that we're not dealing with people here. They *used* to be people. But they've forgotten all about that."

"They're still people, Jalel," Noah said quietly.

"Preacher-man, I've heard about you," Jalel said as he sat down. "You think God's going to destroy the world, but you keep trying to take everybody with you." He laughed. "But I want to tell you something: You don't want to take the Demon pack with you. Do you know what they did to the men who were guarding your son? They're so evil they even scare the other packs. They do things for pleasure that you and I have never even heard of.

"They take someone. They mutilate that person until he cries out to be killed. Do you understand? People that want to live end up begging the pack to kill them because they just can't stand any more pain and mutilation. And they don't just mutilate people; they make the people *watch* as they're being mutilated."

Jalel shook his head sadly.

"The only thing as bad as the mutilation is never being able to forget it."

As Jalel proceeded to describe the details of several Demon pack mutilations, Noah felt immobilized by the unbelievable violence.

"Please, Jalel, please stop."

"I just want you to know what we're dealing with here."

"I know," Noah said weakly. "I can't believe it, but I know. I just can't listen to it anymore."

"All right. But remember I warned you. Do you still want to go ahead?"

"Yes. I want you to make preparations for this, and be fully ready to go to work when you find him. But I want to go along when you make the rescue."

"No!" Jalel protested. "I don't take others along."

"This time you'll have to," Noah insisted. "I'm going to be there. If my son lives, I'm going to be there to see his face. If my son dies, I'm going to be there to die with him."

"Hmmm," Jalel said. He thought about the idea for several minutes. "I don't know why you want to go," he said finally, "but for some reason I think I'm going to agree." He looked intently at Noah. "I've heard from many that you're a fool," he said, "but nobody ever told me that you're a brave fool."

Noah smiled. "I *am* a fool, Jalel. But I'm God's fool. I'm an object of laughter and scorn to everyone in the region—maybe in the world. It would be easy to give in. But I'd rather be God's fool than their leader."

The big man laughed. "Well said!" He looked at Noah with an odd sort of admiration. "I'm a fool, too. People can't understand why I'd risk my life to save others. They think I'm a fool." He slowly stroked his moustache. "You know, when you think about it, we're both in the same business, you and I. We both try to save people."

"And we're both fools," Noah said, smiling.

Jalel laughed again. "Yes! But I don't really think you're a fool. I think you may have some things figured out. Things *are* pretty bad. How can a world full of Demon packs go on? I've lived a long time and I've seen how far down things have gone. That's why I know there's . . . some kind of end coming. That's why I want to get on that ship with you."

Noah was completely surprised. "What?"

"I want to get on that thing at the right time. I don't know what you see coming, but I want to miss it."

Noah was pleased but so surprised that he was uncertain how to respond. "Does this . . . does this mean that you believe what I shared about God with you earlier?"

Now Jalel looked surprised. "What? Oh, no. I don't believe all that. I don't fear God, but I do fear . . . something."

Noah nodded. "I understand that fear, Jalel, but I'm still not sure what you're telling me."

"I'm telling you this. I *don't* want to believe in your God, but I *do* want to get on that ship."

Noah had never before even considered this possibility. *I've always looked at the two ideas as a group he thought. You either believe God for eternal life and get in the box for safety, or you didn't believe God and laughed at the box.* "Let me understand this," he said slowly. "You don't believe God, but you still want to get on the ship?"

"That's it," the big man agreed. "You can think of it as being prepared for all situations. I get to live my life the way I want to, but I get on that thing at the right time and get to go on living while these others die."

Noah was deeply troubled. "Jalel, I have to tell you, I don't know if that will work."

"What? Why not?"

"I don't think you can have it both ways. I don't think you can reject God's plan for your life and still expect Him to protect you from His judgment."

Jalel furrowed his brow.

"Are you telling me I can't get on?" he asked, with an edge to his voice.

Noah nodded uncertainly.

"I think so."

Jalel was angry. "I'm not sure I'm going to give you a choice," he said sharply. "I may make it part of the price of rescuing your son."

Noah felt like he needed this man, but he didn't want to agree with his request. He searched for something to say. Could it be that God wanted him to take this man with him and hope for him to come to God later? When Noah wasn't sure about a decision, he always looked for time. "Jalel," he said finally, "you haven't found Shem yet. I agree to your price, but I'm not sure about your request to come with us. Please give me time to think about it."

Jalel seemed satisfied with this.

"Agreed," he said. He led Noah to the door of his ascetic living space. "One more thing," he said as he opened the door. "If your son's been mutilated when we find him, do you still want him alive?"

Noah was shocked at the question. "I can't believe you're asking me that. I want my son back, however he is."

"Many have said that," the big man said with a measure of severity, "and then have changed their minds when they saw what had been done to the person."

"That's the difference between what I believe and what you believe," Noah responded. "You think that if he's mutilated, that's the end. But I believe that he's still valuable and important, even if he *is* mutilated and stays that way. But Jalel, I believe a lot more than that."

"What's that?"

"I believe that he might be brutalized, but my God can make him whole again. Even if he's *dead,* God can make him whole again."

Jalel laughed but stopped when he saw that Noah was serious. "I think you must really believe that," he said.

"I do," Noah said firmly as he walked out the door. As he left the building, he prayed for Shem, and that God would prepare Tess's heart for what he had to share.

🙿 🙿 🙿

"I *do* accept Him," Kedrah said, tears filling her eyes. "Thank you God!"

"Amen," Tess agreed, shivering with emotion. "This is a great day for you, Kedrah — and for me."

"Why for you?" Kedrah asked.

Tess pulled her close, hugged her, and patted her on the back. "Because, my dear friend, you've become God's friend. If you really mean what you just said, nothing can ever tear you away from Him."

"I *do* mean it," Kedrah said with conviction.

"I can sense that you really do," Tess agreed as she took Kedrah's hand. "I want to do everything I can to help you get closer to God. If you'd like, we can study the Code together."

"I'd like that," Kedrah said eagerly. "I especially need to know how to live with my husband. I don't know how he'll react when he finds out what I now believe. But I'm really glad that I believe it, Tess. Thank you."

Tess began crying. "God is so good, Kedrah. You and I have talked about this for so long, and yet He works out the timing for when . . ."

"Please go on," Kedrah gently urged.

"Oh, Kedrah, you know that my Shem is gone! But watching you come to God — it just reminds me once again how real God is and how much He cares for us."

Kedrah now hugged Tess. "I'm glad it was today, friend," she whispered. "For you and for me."

🙿 🙿 🙿

As Noah went home in his transport, he was absorbed in his thoughts about his family. Shem was in the hands of an unbelievably evil group; Noah was struggling with doubts that he would ever see his son alive again. Ham was now overdue on his return from his trip to Nod, and Noah grieved over letting Ham go to that degenerate place. Japheth was still recovering from his beating by the Nephilim. And Tess had withdrawn more and more, discouraged and depressed by the load.

He thought about what he would say to her when he got home. He knew he couldn't share anything about the Demon pack itself. She would be sick with fear, even worse than she was already. He went through his words to her over and over again in his mind. "I give it to you, God," he prayed. "I can't say these things to the broken woman I left at home this morning."

ta ta ta

As he sped down the pathway near the project, he was shaken out of his thoughts by the sight of flames rising over the hill. He quickly turned around and went back to the private pathway that led to the project. As he drove over the hill, he could see that the east end of the ship was on fire.

He lifted the voice-sender from his control panel. "Meta," he shouted.

"Yes?" a voice answered.

"Meta, we've got a fire! Get everybody to the east end of the ship right now!"

Noah drove his transport through the gate and to the project. He could see Meta directing all of the workers to that area. Several workers were pointing the high-impact waterchannels in the direction of the fire.

About two hours later, the fire out and darkness setting in, Noah slumped down next to Meta.

"God was gracious," Noah said. "The damage could have been a lot worse."

"I don't know if I'd call that *gracious*," Meta said without moving his head. "If that's gracious, then I can't take any more of it. In fact, I *can't* take any more of it."

"What are you saying?" Noah asked, greatly concerned.

"I'm saying I'm through." He looked at Noah. "I'm through. I can't take it. It's been too hard on my family and too hard on my friendships. And it's just become too dangerous—even at the high rates of pay you've given me."

Noah's head dropped. "I understand, Meta. But what will I do?"

"You've got Dainea," he said slowly. "She's good, and she seems fearless."

Noah didn't speak for several minutes. "Will you stay on for a while?" he asked finally.

Meta looked at him. "You've been fair with me. I don't understand you, but you've been fair with me. I don't want to stay. I want to get as far away from here as possible. But I'll stay for one more week to help Dainea take over the project."

"Thank you," Noah said appreciatively as he patted Meta on the back.

Meta stood up and walked away. Gradually everyone but Noah left the project. The site for once was strangely silent. Noah had never felt so alone.

He leaned back and looked at the moon through the distant water canopy. "I know You're up there, Lord," he prayed. "Please help me to know that You're down here, too."

And Noah, the comforter, was comforted by his God.

CHAPTER 17

As he looked through the window of the airship at the ground below, Noah thought back to the conversation he'd had the day before with Nusheela.

She had come to him reluctantly, at the urging of Sicilee. "Noah," she had said, "I have to speak with you."

He had smiled and taken her hand. "I didn't even know that you and Ham were back."

She had looked away. "We're . . . he's . . . he's *not* back. He wouldn't come with me." He remembered the fear in her eyes when she had looked at him.

"What happened?" Noah had asked, concern filling his voice.

Nusheela had begun crying. "He was . . . he did well at first. He worked hard during the day and came to our room at night. And then one night—he just didn't come back at all. I went to look for him and I saw him . . . with one of those women!"

Nusheela had cried for a long time.

She had asked Noah to bring her husband home. Even before she had asked, he had desired in his heart to do that very thing. But he'd also struggled during the night, asking God what he should do.

Noah felt sick that he had allowed Ham to go, even with Nusheela, but he knew that the serpent had caught his own heart in a moment of grief and weakness after Shem had been stolen.

Noah regretted having yielded to his human frailty especially since he had known for so many years about the vulnerability to spiritual at-

tacks that often came with grief and fear. He asked God to keep him
from making any more major decisions when such attacks came.

During the night he had finally realized that if Ham had left home
intending to sin and run away from God, Noah wouldn't be able to bring
him back. In that situation, he would have to leave Ham in the hands of
God. But he had felt in his heart that Ham had left intending to be
faithful to Nusheela and had fallen into sin. With that in mind, he knew
he had to try to find his lost son.

And now here he was, speeding through the water canopy in one of
the largest airships ever built, traveling toward one of the world's great
centers of sin, Tep-Gsepdotdu in the land of Nod.

He remembered his first time in this awesome city, when he had
come as a little boy with his father. Even then, 590 years before, a
visitor knew that there was something wrong, something evil about the
place. It was a place for wanderers, those without roots and without
principles. Even then, it was a center of business and trade. There were
some things that you couldn't find at a good price and in quantity unless
you came here.

Noah hated the region of Nod, and this, its largest city. He had always hated it. As the airship touched the ground, he felt even greater
remorse at ever sending his youngest son to the infamous "den of pleasures."

Even though it was very late, the city was teeming with life. Loud,
wild music came from all directions as he traveled in the rented transport to his room. Every corner of the city seemed full of prostitutes and
people in obscene embraces. Terrible images and statues were everywhere. In just a few minutes Noah saw four fights.

It had been said for many years that if you wanted something, no
matter what it was, you could find it in Tep-Gsepdotdu. *And many
things you would never want, too,* Noah thought to himself.

He got to his lodging house and went to the housemaster.

"Name?" the man behind the counter said without interest.

"Noah Seth-Lamech."

"Forty-fifth level," the man responded "Man or woman?"

Noah didn't understand. "What?"

"Man or woman?" the strange man replied.

"I don't know what you're talking about."

"I want to know what you want in your room, a man or a woman."

Noah finally understood. "Let me tell you something," he said angrily. "I can't believe that you're just asking that, as though it's normal — not even in this city. But you keep your 'men and women' away from me — unless they want to hear about God."

The man laughed. "God never comes to Nod," he said sarcastically.

Noah stared at him. "That'd be your loss, if it were true, because nobody can really live without God. But He *is* coming to Nod, and that *will* be your loss. Someday soon there'll be nothing left of this miserable place, except what exists in a few memories. And if God is gracious, He'll wipe out the memories, too."

The man grinned. "You're a sick man," he said in even tones. "Enjoy your stay in Tep-Gsep."

Noah went up to his room, put down his clothesbox, and went to the window. He looked out on the incredible lights and buildings that made up the heart of the city, and marveled at what Cain had accomplished in the land of Nod. Cain had built a teeming empire, full of wealth and power and sin. Just as Cain had carried a mark from God, so this city carried a mark from Cain — the mark of sin and death.

Something in him wanted to get right out into the city, but something else told him to take time, pray, and think. He decided to clean up and change clothes before he started his search for Ham.

As he looked in the reflector, it struck him that the amount of gray in his beard had increased greatly. He laughed and prayed that God would keep him from trying to carry the load that he knew only God could carry.

Noah finally went out, just after the twentieth hour of the day. Noise — transports, walking marketers, shouting, laughing — dominated the central sector of the city. Noah turned to his right and started to thread his way through the dense crowds of people.

Nusheela had told him where she thought Ham would be. Noah walked steadily toward that area, just two thousand cubits from the lodging house where he was staying. He prayed that he would be able to find Ham quickly, and not use up valuable time that could be spent working on the box.

His prayers were answered. As he went around a corner, he sensed that his son was near. And then, almost immediately, he felt that his son was in great danger. He prayed again, for wisdom and courage to face the thing that was lurking in the evil places just ahead.

He had tried to dress in such a way that he wouldn't draw attention, but people stopped to stare at him as he walked past. He couldn't shake the feeling that somehow he was expected.

He saw a man leaning against a pathlight. Noah felt repulsed and yet drawn to him at the same time.

"Greetings," Noah said cheerfully. "How are you?" The man grunted. "Can you tell me," Noah continued, "if you've seen a young man named Ham Seth-Noah?"

The man laughed perversely. "So you're the man," he said with a confidence that shook Noah.

"What do you mean?" Noah asked.

"I mean, 'so you're the man,' just like I said," the man said sharply. "Yes, Ham Seth-Noah is here. He said you'd come. We've been looking forward to meeting the builder of 'Noah's folly.'" The man grinned. "Did you know that your fame had even reached Tep-Gsep?"

Noah took a deep breath. "No, I hadn't. When I was younger, I always thought I wanted to be well known. But I hadn't planned to become well known as a fool."

The man laughed. "But you are! You're one of the most famous people in the region — maybe even in the whole world. Everybody knows about the funny preacher who builds funny ships."

"I build funny ships because the world isn't such a funny place anymore." Noah said sadly.

"Oh, oh, I can smell a preacher."

"What if it's not just a strange idea?" Noah persisted. "What if I'm right? What if the wrath of God really is coming?"

The man frowned at Noah. "I think I've changed my mind. I don't think you're funny at all. I think you're sick."

"Perhaps I am," Noah said sadly. "But even a sick man ought to get to see his son. Will you tell me where he is?"

The man studied Noah's face. "The preacher with the wild son. Very interesting." Suddenly, the man stood up straight and started walking. "I'll do better than tell you," he shouted. "I'll take you to him."

Noah followed the man into a gaudy drug center. The main room was full of people who were drinking, inhaling, and absorbing into their arms and legs a variety of drugs. Some laughed as he walked past. Others sneered. Some were too controlled by the drugs to even notice him.

As they approached the corner, Noah's heart sank. He could see Ham, almost unconscious, sitting at a table with several men and women. "Well, not-so-funny preacher, here's your son!" Noah's guide said sarcastically.

Noah stood at the edge of the table and looked intently at his son. "Ham," he said just loudly enough to be heard, "it's time for you to come home."

Everyone at the table laughed. "He sounds just like I thought he would," an immodestly dressed woman said in a slurred voice.

"Sit up, Ham," another woman said as she pushed on his arm. "Can't you see that your daddy is here? Don't you have any respect?"

"Ah, do . . . I can't . . ." Ham was trying, but couldn't say anything.

Noah realized that Ham was so drunk that conversation would be impossible. "If you'll excuse me," Noah said as he moved around the table, "I'll just take my son home and let you go on with your . . . lives."

When he drew near to Ham, he felt a large hand come down on his shoulder. He turned to face the man who had led him into the room.

The man's face was red with anger. "You're not taking him anywhere, daddy Noah," the man said in a mocking voice. "We like your son. He has a lot of money. He buys us things. He belongs to us now."

"Are you telling me you're not going to let me take my son home?" Noah asked quietly.

"More than that, big man. I'm telling you to turn around and get out of here or you're going to go home—*dead.*"

Noah prayed quickly for strength. He reached down and pulled Ham to his feet, and then spoke to the sinister man standing in his way. "This is my son," he said, in a voice that was still quiet, but also strong and powerful—even intimidating. "My son belongs to God, and he belongs to me. The only thing that belongs to you is misery and death." He started to pull Ham forward. "I'm taking my son home."

"Don't try to stop me," he warned, as he looked intently into the man's eyes.

Suddenly, one of the people behind Noah pulled Ham out of Noah's grip. As Noah turned to watch his son fall, he heard the man who had blocked his exit curse.

Noah turned back to see a fist coming at his face. He grabbed the man's hand, stepped aside, and threw the man against the wall. He hit the wall hard and slumped against it.

Noah turned quickly to see another man rushing at him. Once again, Noah stepped aside, grabbed the man's arm, and threw him against the wall. This second attacker fell to the floor just as the first man had gotten back to his feet.

Noah went to the first man and pushed him against the wall. "Do you understand?" he asked, loudly enough for others nearby to hear. "Do you understand? I don't want to—God knows I don't want to—but in the power of God I could kill you right now."

Although those in the room were used to fights, this man's intensity was so unusual that everyone became quiet. "You can't kill us all," one of the men sitting at Ham's table said fiercely.

Noah looked around at him. "You're right. I can't kill you all. I don't really *want* to kill you all." He looked back at the man in his grip. "I don't even want to kill you. I'll leave you to God. I just want my son. I'm going to take him home now."

He let the man go, went to Ham, picked him up, and started walking. "You can attack me," he said, looking around. "You might even kill me. And you'll have to, if you want to stop me. But think about this: Some of you might die too. Is it worth it?"

Noah prayed, almost screaming inside for God to help. He knew that there was no possibility of making it through the door without God's restraining hand on all of the men, and even the women. Any one of them could attack him and kill him. The fear was almost overwhelming, but Noah continued to pray and to thank God for hearing him.

Just after the second hour of the new day, having made plans for his sick son to return home on a medical airship, Noah went to his lodging house and fell asleep praising God for His great deliverance.

CHAPTER 18

"I just don't know if we're all going to live to get in the box," Tess, working on endday meal, said with great frustration.

Noah watched her as she cut several large melons. "Be careful, or we'll have some of *you* in tonight's meal," he teased.

She turned to face him. "You," she said, brushing back her hair and looking at the cutter in her hand, "you . . ." She turned back to her work. "It isn't funny," she insisted.

Noah knew this was the time to persist. He got up, walked behind her, and gave her a hug. "But if we don't laugh," he whispered into her ear, "we'll spend all of our time angry and crying."

"I *want* to spend all of my time angry and crying," she said without turning around.

"All right," he said, letting go of her and leaning back against the workspace next to her. "All right. Let me hear it all."

"You want to hear it all?" she asked, not looking up from her work. "I'll tell you. My family is falling apart. Japheth and you are attacked and beaten. Shem . . . Shem is stolen from us, and we don't know where he is. Ham goes away . . . and comes back sick, diseased. I hate it!"

He could see that she was crying. He reached up and brushed away several tears. "I hate it, too," he said softly.

"Oh, I know you do," she said, tears flowing down her face. "I know that. I just don't know what we can do about it."

"Let me tell you something that will help," he encouraged as he took her hand. "God spoke to me very strongly today about our Shem.

He told me that someone great will descend from him." He turned her face toward him. "Tess, I think it could be the serpent-slayer."

"You think we . . ." Tess stopped to wipe her face.

"I think we'll get him back," Noah finished her thought. "Tess, this is a time of great trial for us. But how could we have ever expected it to be easy? We're standing against everything around us. But we'll get him back, Tess. I don't know how it will work out, but God does. I just know we'll get him back."

She came to him and hugged him tightly. "I hope you're right," she said, her face buried in his chest.

                ❧ ❧ ❧

"I don't want to live," Ham, looking away from his father, said with great discouragement.

Noah looked tenderly at the young man lying on the bed in the healing center. "You have much to live for," he encouraged.

"I have nothing to live for," Ham insisted. "I lose either way. If what you say doesn't happen, we'll all be laughed at as fools for the rest of our lives. If it does happen, everything I've grown up with and learned to care about will be gone." He put his hands over his face. "I can be a fool or I can be alone. It's too much. I can't take it."

"Son," Noah said cautiously, "it *is* going to happen. You know that. . . ."

Ham looked around at his father. "I don't know anything. And either way, I'm sick because of . . ." His voice trailed off as he looked away from his father.

"You can tell me," Noah prodded gently.

"I'm sick because of some liar that gave me an infected—" He caught himself. "I made a mistake. That's all."

"It wasn't just a mistake," Noah persisted. "It was a sin."

"And now I have to die?" Ham said as he flashed an angry look at his father. "Look at all the people that spend their lives in . . . that way. They don't have to die. I spend a few weeks there, and they tell me I'm going to die. What kind of a God allows that?"

Noah sat down next to his son. "Don't blame God, Ham. Sins have consequences. But if you repent and ask God to forgive you, perhaps He'll be gracious and heal your sickness as well."

"I don't believe . . . I don't believe those things anymore."

"Ham, please . . ."

"Dad," Ham said, pulling his coverings up near his mouth, "please leave me alone. I'm going to die. I just want to be left alone. Can't you understand that I don't want to think about those things right now?"

Noah realized that he could make no further progress with his youngest son. He squeezed his arm and then stood up to leave. Standing over the bed, he prayed that his son would seek God's forgiveness and mercy. He wanted to touch him but made himself leave the room.

He went down several levels and came to Japheth's room. As the door slid closed behind him, he heard a hearty "Hi, Dad!" from across the room.

"Peace to you," Noah responded cheerfully. He walked over to where Japheth was resting. Most of the wrappings had been removed from his head and face, but ugly bruises ran from his chin to his forehead. Although his right eye had been worked on for seven hours by the doctors, they still were uncertain about how well he would be able to see. The Nephilim had done his work too well.

"I'm . . . I'm feeling better, Dad," Japheth offered, trying to sound positive. "I don't know about this eye, but the rest of me is getting better."

"I really feel that your eye is going to get better, too," Noah encouraged as he sat down close to his son.

"I never had anything hurt so much as when that Nephilim hit me in the eye—except for when you spanked me that time I put rotten grapes on Mom's seat and she sat on them!" They both laughed.

"They're going to make me leave," Noah said, trying to hold back the laughter. "We've got to stop making so much noise. You know, I remember that—" His eyes caught Japheth's, and they both started laughing again.

"Dad," Japheth asked after they finally quieted down, "will you tell me the truth? Didn't you and Mom think at the time that I was just a little funny?"

"Japheth, I can't tell you how many times your mother and I have laughed ourselves to sleep remembering that story. But we couldn't let you think you were as funny as *you* thought you were."

"I'll remember that when I have a son," Japheth said with a smile. He put his hand on his father's hand. "Dad, how's Ham?"

Noah shook his head. "He's really bitter. Something about losing Shem just took out his heart. And now the doctors have told him that there's no hope."

Japheth looked very concerned. "We'd better keep a family vigil if they've told him that. You know how so many of these doctors are now. Once they've given up hope of a complete healing, they can take away needed care, even food and water. They like to sweep their 'failures' out of the way."

Noah nodded in agreement. "You're right, of course. I still think they went even further with Naamah's first son. I think they did something to end his life."

Japheth pushed himself to a more upright position. "They seem to think if you're dying, there's no point in living."

"And what they miss is the fact that we're *all* dying," Noah added. "Many people don't look like they're dying, but we all are. Everyone just seems to look harder at the ones who *look* like they're dying."

"When we make our new start," Japheth said as he poured a drink, "I hope we can build into the next generation the belief that all life is precious, even if it only has a few hours to live."

"Yes!" Noah agreed enthusiastically. "And we can hope that never again will people make life so cheap that they take it away just because it becomes a problem or a burden. May a day of violence and disrespect for life such as ours never darken the new earth as it has this one."

"Do you know what I think?" Japheth asked, squinting his good eye. "I think that if people ever fall to this level again, God'll judge them just like he's judging our generation. Maybe not with a flood, but with some kind of judgment."

Japheth looked up to see Sicilee enter the room. "If people in a region won't put a stop to the violence, then I think God will put a stop to the region," he concluded, smiling at her.

"I can see that I've come into a very serious conversation," Sicilee said, smiling at both men. "What have I missed?"

Japheth laughed. "Well, I'm not sure how we got off on that path, but we ended up talking about how we want to raise the next generation to have more respect for life than our has."

"I think we started in that direction by talking about the doctors' future care of Ham," Noah recalled.

Sicilee looked angry. "Tess told me this morning that the doctors have said he's going to . . . I just can't believe it."

"Believe it," Japheth responded. "We were just agreeing that it's time to begin a family vigil, to make sure that he's cared for and not harmed."

"I want to be there as much as I can," Sicilee said with conviction. "I want to keep praying for him, and serving him, and doing what I can to encourage him."

Noah's face softened as he listened to her. "Thank you, daughter," he said with deep affection. "Your love and care for him, and for the whole family, is so very special. You're a real treasure to me."

She took Noah's hand and looked into his eyes. "And *you're* a real treasure to me." She looked at Japheth and then back at Noah. "I've told this to Japheth, but now I'd like to tell you. Even though my own father is dead, I have a father who is also my dear friend."

She squeezed Noah's hand. "It's you. You were the one God used to bring me back to Him. Being close to you brings me closer to God. I'm grateful to Him, and I'm grateful to you. I'm just so glad that God has bound our two spirits into one."

"May it always be so for us," Noah added. "I feel the same way about you—that God has given me a true daughter along with my sons, a special friend for the rest of our days together. And I know that if anyone can lift Ham's spirit right now, it's you."

"I agree," Japheth said, leaning forward to pat her on the leg. "I wish I could do more. I know I can really bother him at times, but I really love him. Dad, I've never shared this with you before, but I want to now. When Ham was a little boy, all he wanted to do was go wherever I went and do whatever I did. And I'd call him names and tell him to go away."

Japheth's voice choked with emotion. "Even after all these years, I can still see that scrawny little boy with the funny little face, crying when I'd treat him that way."

"I'll try to help him know how you feel about him," Sicilee said gently.

"I just wish I could wipe away all of those times, all of those tears," Japheth said, sadness filling his voice.

"God can wipe them away, and bring you closer to each other," she encouraged. After a brief silence, she continued. "I also want to confess something. I know my heart hasn't always been committed to the work. But God has shown me that even if I don't understand everything, I can trust those he's placed in my life to guide and protect me.

"I know now that I can trust you two as husband and spiritual father, as those in authority in my life for God. I know now that being under authority isn't a burden; it's the way to freedom. I'm sorry I ever doubted you, or kept myself from full commitment."

The three of them took hands. They each prayed in turn for Ham and Shem, and pledged themselves to God, each other, and the work.

CHAPTER 19

T he light on the voice-sender had been flashing for several minutes before Noah looked up from his final design changes and noticed it. He had turned off the sound to avoid interruption.

Now he walked to the table and touched a presspoint. "Yes?" he asked.

"This is Jalel," the man said, his gruff voice filling the room. Noah made an adjustment to the sound level. "We've been contacted by the pack who took your son," Jalel continued.

"Is he . . ."

"He's still alive," Jalel said matter-of-factly. "You're too rich and he's too valuable for them to kill him yet. They've set the redemption amount."

"How much?" Noah asked, with surprising joy growing in his heart as he realized his hopes for his son had not been ended.

"Fifty thousand darmas, plus your agreement to burn your ship."

"What?"

"You heard me. They want money, but they also want you to destroy your project."

Noah sat down. "The money is one thing," he said weakly, "but this other thing . . ."

"It doesn't matter," Jalel said abruptly, "because we're not going to deal with them anyway. They told me that if they don't have an answer in twenty-four hours, they're going to maim him, molest him, and inject him with an altered, deadly life-form. People who would even think about doing things like that aren't going to just let him go."

"Dear God," Noah breathed.

"I don't know about God," Jalel grunted, "but I do know about Nephilim. They said they were going to let the Nephilim loose in a room with him. Seth-Lamech, they don't just kill people anymore."

Noah felt sick. "What are you planning?" Noah asked, praying that God would help him control his fear.

"I've spent a lot of time on this," Jalel answered. "I already know that this pack is holding him in one of four places, all very close to each other. I have men watching each one of them. We can't be around when they pick up our response, but I know the approximate time they're going to pick it up—tonight, in the middle of the night. My men'll be watching to see who enters one of those places shortly after the response has been picked up. That should tell us where they are."

Noah felt sick. "What if that isn't the place?"

"You mean what if I'm wrong?" Jalel asked. "Well, if we take this approach and attack the wrong place, your son is in trouble."

"What are we going to say in the response?" said Noah, searching for something to say.

"We're going to tell them that we agree. We'll have to include five thousand darmas to show good faith since they'll probably open the response before we get there. Before we have to pay the rest, I hope we'll already have your son."

"I'll have the five thousand ready in two hours," Noah said. "Should I meet you at your office?"

"Yes. Just remember that you agreed to stay out of the way when we make the rescue."

Noah agreed and turned off the voice-sender. After he finished his preparations, he selected a memorypack from the many shelves along the wall in his office. He went to the lower level and looked for Tess, before remembering that she had gone to buy more clothes for storage in the box. He got into his transport and entered the memorypack into the viewlife.

"This is Adam," he heard before looking down to see the face of his ancestor. "I want to share with you today something that many have asked me about. I do this with a heart full of sadness and eyes full . . ."

Noah glanced down, and even though the image was faded, he could see tears streaming down Adam's cheeks.

"I've been asked to speak about the first mur . . . about the death of my son Abel. People want to know how such a thing could have happened. I think they want to know so they can stop such a thing from happening in their own families.

"I don't really know how to answer this question. I feel the same when I'm asked about the first sin . . . about the time when I yielded my spirit to the serpent. There I was, standing there, looking at that glorious fruit from the incredible tree of knowledge. I was drawn toward it, I wanted it, I wanted to believe that eating it would give me knowledge like God.

"But I knew in my spirit that it was a lie. *I knew it!* I knew there was only one God, and that my knowledge could never be like His. What I know, I can only really know because God shares it with me. What I learn any other way only—always—leads to destruction and death.

"I stood there, holding not just a piece of fruit, but everyone who would ever live in the palm of my hand. I should have thrown it away, instead of throwing away the joy of sinlessness for everyone else for the rest of time."

There was a pause. Noah looked down to see Adam looking away, filled with grief.

"I've shared this with you," Adam said, "so you'll know why I'm going to say only a few things about Abel's death. Cain's failure is largely my failure. My sin opened the door to Cain's sin. And even though I was forgiven, I didn't feel I had the right to judge Cain or discipline him as a boy. I had the wisdom and power from God to raise him to be a godly young man, but I didn't do it. Yes, it's his fault; but it's my fault, too.

"I knew Cain hated Abel, but I tried to ignore it, I tried to deal with it with speeches about love. I didn't get into Cain's heart. I let him say things to Abel that should have been punished. I was wrong. . . ."

Noah turned his transport into the area in front of Jalel's office. Stopping the transport, he looked intently into the image.

". . . totally wrong. Eve and I didn't see the truth about the importance of our position with Cain. Please don't make the same mistake with your children.

"And now I'll say only one more thing about this. When I think of that time, the only image that comes to my mind is a field of sacrifice. Eve had told me . . . that Abel had gone out with Cain and was hours late, and I went out to find him. I went to the place where he sacrificed to God, to be cleansed of his sins and to honor the coming serpent-slayer.

"And there he was, lying on the ground with blood all around him—his own precious blood! I stopped and fell to my knees, and all I could see was that beautiful face, beaten and broken. That, and a piece of fruit next to him on the ground.

"I picked up the fruit, and I saw in my hand a reminder of that long-ago piece of fruit that I should have thrown away. I stood up and threw this one away, as far as I could. And then I fell back to the ground and picked my . . . my son's head up and held it in my arms. I sat on the ground, rocking back and forth, holding him and crying, for hours and hours.

"I'll never really stop crying until I hold him in my arms again."

Noah didn't know why he had picked this memorypack, but he knew that God had directed him to it. And Noah cried with Adam, until Adam's image was gone.

&a &a &a

"It's getting close," Jalel said to Noah, who was sitting next to him in the dark transport.

"I have no strength left," Noah said, looking forward.

Jalel looked at Noah and smiled. "I still can't believe that you wanted to be here."

"I *have* to be here. I have no choice. If I have to, I'll die with him."

"If all of this works out," Jalel encouraged, "the pack will die and your son will live."

Noah looked at Jalel. "Jalel, I don't care if the pack dies today or not. I think they're going to be dead in three weeks anyway. All I care about today is my son."

"Understand this," Jalel admonished him. "If we don't kill the pack, we don't get your son. That's the *only* way we'll get him."

A light on the power panel began to go on and off. "What's that mean?" Noah asked.

"That's it," Jalel said with excitement. "It's number three. Somebody's just gone into number three."

Jalel hurriedly started the transport and moved away quickly. After driving for about three minutes, he stopped on a quiet pathway between two large houses. He turned to Noah. "That big one there is it," he said, pointing. "I'm going up there, but I want you to stay here until I come for you. Understand?"

Noah nodded. He watched as Jalel silently moved into the lush plant life that filled the pathway. He heard and saw nothing for almost fifteen minutes. He prayed for Shem, and for peace in his own heart.

Finally, he heard several screams. He got out of the transport and began to run toward the house.

He came to the front window, looked through, and saw nothing. He went around to the side of the house and again saw nothing through the first-level window. A flash of light from the lower-level window caught his attention, and he bent down to look.

His heart, already pounding, went wild. He saw Jalel, his face bleeding, standing before a raging Nephilim. Jalel held a huge cutter in his hand, and seemed to be taunting the monster to attack him. Two of Jalel's men were fighting with four members of the pack at the other end of the large room. Noah began to pray furiously.

And then he looked to the left and saw his son. His heart leapt with joy. But he saw two men kneeling near Shem's head, one of them holding a piercing tube. Noah knew at once that it was the deadly life-form.

As Noah watched, the Nephilim advanced against Jalel, and Jalel began to slash back and forth with his cutter, opening huge wounds in the rampaging giant. When he grabbed Jalel's arm and threw Jalel to the ground, Noah jumped up and began to look feverishly for a way into the house.

He stumbled, running along the back of the house and trying to feel his way. He finally found a broken door and went in. The entryway was totally dark.

He heard a scream and ran in the direction of the sound. As he walked into the large room, the sight overwhelmed him.

There were bodies everywhere. In the center of the room, in a huge heap, the Nephilim lay dead. Pack members had been decimated by Jalel's relentless men, but several of them lay motionless on the ground as well.

Noah looked in the direction of his son and felt a hand drop on his shoulder. "We did what we could," he heard Jalel saying.

Noah's felt dizzy. "Is he . . ."

"He's not dead. But they've beaten him pretty badly and broken his nose. And we couldn't keep them from piercing him with . . ." Jalel shook his head and walked over to where his men were tending to their fallen friends.

Now Noah knew why he had listened to Adam. Noah stumbled over to his son and dropped to the ground. He picked up the piercing tube and threw it to the other end of the room. Lifting his son's head into his arms, Noah rocked back and forth, holding him and crying, for hours and hours.

CHAPTER 20

Noah was awed by the fury of the activity.

The number of people working on the project was at its peak, and the exterior of the ship was almost finished. Several groups were working around the large door. Others were working on the upper level, finishing the ship to within a cubit of the top. The vented windows were already being put in place on the third level.

He saw Japheth standing inside the door, giving directions to several workers who were finishing the cages on the first level. He had only been back on the project for three days, but his presence was already being felt. The doctors had concluded that he would never see again out of his damaged eye, but even that hadn't dampened his spirit.

Noah saw Japheth begin to walk up the ramp that led to the second level. There, Noah knew, the workers would be unloading and storing the boxes of food that were being hoisted in by a power-lift. Many boxes at a time were being swung through the hole that had been left in the side of the ship at that level. Some of them contained seeds, plants, and small trees, all of which Noah intended to use in the new earth.

And Noah had an image of Tess and the other women working on the top level to make it a home. Several groups of rooms had been built for each family, with a common area for large family meals and sharing. The women had been working on placement of clothes and other supplies in the huge cedar storage rooms.

Early in the project Noah had decided not to take very much equipment on the box. He knew that there would be nothing in the new world to use as a power source, and equipment that had its own source would need spare parts that at some point would run out and not be replaceable.

Because of this, Noah had become a collector of old, manually operated equipment and machinery. Some items had been out of use for many years and were very difficult to find. In a few cases, he'd even had to pay a craftsman to build something from old images and drawings. He had once spent two days trying to find enough information to make a simple flour mill.

He laughed as he remembered the look on Tess's face when he had brought home a foot-powered sewing machine, and her comment that she would never use anything like that. And then he remembered how he had felt when he had missed her in the night, and had come quietly down to the first level to stand in the shadows and watch her humming joyously while she used the funny old machine.

He was also taking basic tools that a small group of people could use in farming and building. He had included a substantial amount of raw materials, including some refined metals that would be difficult or impossible to produce in quantity after the box landed.

He had decided to take as much in the way of finished goods as they could afford and find room to store. They had so much to do, building a life from a new beginning, that he knew they wouldn't have time to make everything for themselves.

He had included a large library in the common area on the third level, even though he knew that the books were not reproducible, that they wouldn't last, and that much of the knowledge wouldn't be immediately usable and would probably be lost over time.

He smiled as he thought of one of the books—the one he had written on the coming judgment and the need to repent. He had been unable to find anyone to issue it, and so he had spent his own money to make and send out twenty thousand copies to people in all parts of the earth.

"I never knew you wanted to be famous as a writer," Tess had teased him.

"I don't," Noah had said, smiling. "I only want to be famous with God. And I don't want to have anyone's blood on my hands."

"Then I have another idea," she had said. "Let's find a way to spread the word even more."

And so, with her help, he had made a small portion of the book into a short paper, and sent out almost a million copies.

ఎ ఎ ఎ

"Does everybody realize that this project has to be done in two weeks?" Noah asked.

"I understand that very well," Dainea said softly. "When I took this job from Meta, he explained that we were on a timeplan that at some point would become absolute. Two weeks isn't much time, but I think we can do it."

"I'm not so sure," the time-planner said. "Even with the current number of people on the project, and working twenty-four hours a day, my timeplan shows eighteen days of work left. And you say we only have fourteen days to do it."

"Twelve," Dainea said.

"Yes, I've been meaning to talk about that," the time-planner said testily. "I don't understand this at all. We have this project on a wild rush to be finished, and yet we have to stop working every seven days. It doesn't make any sense at all."

"I understand why you don't understand," Noah responded quietly. "It goes back to when God created everything, 1,656 years ago. The Code of Adam says that God made everything in six days, and on the seventh day He rested. He expects the people He made on the sixth day to do no less on the seventh day."

"Strange," the time-planner said in a disbelieving tone.

"It's not for us to judge whether it's strange or not," Dainea responded. "This man is our employer. If he says get the work done in two weeks and wants everyone to rest every seventh day, that's his decision."

"I just think as the project time-planner I have a right to know what the rules are and why," the man said defensively. "I don't understand anything about this project at all. For example, if only a handful of people are going to use it, why does it have to be so big?"

"Because they —" Dainea began.

Noah stopped her with a gesture. "Thank you for trying to defend us, Dainea, but please let me try to explain. In fact, I've never even shared some of this with you. I want you to know everything." He saw her smiling at him, and he smiled back.

"Please go on," Dainea said with great interest.

"Dainea, I've been hoping that you . . . well, I just think you may be someone who decides to get on there with us at the right time."

She nodded. "I have to say that I'm interested. I haven't decided, but I want to hear more."

"Well, this ship is not big because of the number of people we're expecting," Noah explained. "We think there'll be very few, perhaps just ten or twelve. But we think we need to take everything necessary to start life over again. That's why we're putting on so much material and seed and food and other things."

"The top two levels at least make some sense," the time-planner interjected. "It's the bottom level that I don't understand. We're two weeks away from the finish, and there's almost nothing in there."

Noah looked at Japheth, who winked at him. Noah smiled. "What I'm going to tell you now," he said, "will startle you. But it's the truth, and you're going to see it for yourself.

"That level is so large because very soon it's going to be full of animals—of every kind, from every part of the earth."

"What!" the time-planner said, bursting into laughter. "*Animals?*"

Noah laughed too. "Yes, animals. It does sound funny, but in less than two weeks, that entire level is going to be full of every kind of land animal on the face of the earth."

The time-planner was still laughing. "How are you going to feed them all?"

"That's why we're storing food on most of the second level and part of the top level," Noah responded. "I don't know how long we're going to be on that thing, but I'm taking as much food as I have room for."

The time-planner looked full of questions. "But what if you're on it until your food runs out?"

Noah nodded understandingly. "I've thought about that. Do you know what the answer is? I can only do what I can do, and I have to leave the rest to God. But I know this: Before it becomes serious, we'll be where we're supposed to be."

Japheth leaned forward. "He hasn't even asked my favorite questions. Such as 'What about the cleanup?'"

Everyone but the time-planner laughed. "Tell them what I said," Noah encouraged Japheth.

"Dad said that he was bringing shovels and small life-form disintegrators." He touched Dainea on the shoulder. "He said we'd also pray that your ventilation system works, Dainea."

They all laughed again, except for the time-planner, who looked very serious. "I want to know where you're going to get all of these animals. I have nothing in the timeplan to describe it. If we're going to purchase that many animals and get them on in time, I have to know about it today."

"I agree," Dainea said. "I know we have much other work to do, but if that's your desire, we need to take action quickly."

"No need for that, Dainea," Japheth said. "This is where your growing faith is going to be tested. Tell her, Dad."

Noah shifted in his seat. "We don't have to purchase the animals, Dainea. I don't have the money to buy them all, anyway. And it would take months to get that job done, even with large groups working on it."

Noah stood up and walked over to the window. "No, Dainea, I'm not going to do anything, but in two weeks that ship is going to be full of animals."

"Are you . . ." The time-planner was furious. "I can't believe it! We spend all of this time building this project for animals that you haven't even bought? What do you call that?"

"Faith," Japheth said soberly. "Very, very, *very* great faith."

❧ ❧ ❧

"Have one of these," Kedrah said as she handed Tess a handful of grapes.

The few grapes were so large that they filled Tess's hand. "You have one of the most beautiful gardens in the region," Tess said with admiration. It suddenly struck Tess that all of this beauty—all the rich foliage, the exquisite fruits and vegetables, the well-kept garden paths—

would soon be gone. Sorrow filled her heart at the loss of so many good things.

"Things are just not going very well at all," Kedrah said without warning as they finished the walk.

"Is it a problem with . . . Pelenah?" Tess asked cautiously.

"Yes," Kedrah answered. "Ever since I started talking about my new faith, he's just . . . he's been saying such terrible things to me."

They sat down on a white bench in the bright, open-air back room that overlooked Kedrah's breathtaking garden.

"That can be a heavy load," Tess empathized.

"I know you understand about heavy loads, Tess," Kedrah said sympathetically. "With all your challenges right now, I don't know how you can take time to be with me. You're just so . . . special."

"I can only do it because God's carrying my load for me. Sometimes, I have to confess I'm not even sure I'm going to be able to do that small thing and give my loads to God."

Kedrah took her hand. "That's what I see you doing, Tess — giving your loads to God, and somehow still smiling in the midst of things that . . . well, I just appreciate you."

"Is Pelenah only using words to attack you?" Tess asked.

"Well, uh, no." Kedrah paused and looked down at her feet. "Oh, Tess, last night he hit me! He said later he was sorry, but Tess, he hit me! Should I set him aside, Tess?"

Tess shook her head. "No, dear, no. God looks at a lawful marriage as one that lasts for life. That's what He meant when He talked about Adam and Eve and their oneness before Him. The Code — our God — doesn't allow us to set our husbands aside. But if He keeps hitting you, you may have to separate — at least for a while."

"Pray for me, Tess," Kedrah pleaded. "I love him, but sometimes I feel like I . . . like I hate him, too. I know that sounds terrible, but it's the way I feel, Tess. I know you've never felt that way about Noah, but that's because he's a very special man."

Listening to Kedrah talk about Noah made Tess stop and thank God for him in her heart. *Please help him Lord, wherever he is, right now.*

↊ ↊ ↊

"Seth-Lamech?" the man asked gruffly as he came into the project office.

"That's me," said Noah, standing up to face him.

The man frowned. "I'm the regional assistant reviewer. You've already worked with my superior."

"Yes," Noah agreed, remembering that unpleasant encounter. "I think he fined me over a hundred thousand darmas."

"A hundred and fifteen thousand, to be exact."

"And what do you want?"

The man smiled at him. "I've been sent here to review the project again."

"It's been less than nine months!" Japheth protested. "There haven't been any reports that would cause you to come again."

"Let's just say that my superior has a great interest in you and your project."

Noah felt angry. "When will you make your review?"

"I've already finished it."

Noah sat down. "And?"

"And I can't believe that you'd allow so many people to work so rapidly. There's great potential for injury."

Japheth walked up to the man. "Is that all? You make a review, and all you can say is that we have too many people working? We've always taken every possible precaution to protect our workers. And I'd say that every one of those people is glad to be working, especially at the wages we're paying."

"Irrelevant," the man said abruptly. "I'm here to shut down the project."

Noah felt both anger and fear at the same time. "You'd put all of those people out of work?"

"Yes, if we have to." The man came over and sat on the table. "Of course, there *is* another choice."

Noah looked up at him. "A choice? What is it?"

"You can pay a fine."

Noah knew what was coming. "How much?" he asked impatiently.

The man looked down at his records. "Three hundred thousand."

"What do you—" Japheth exploded. Noah stopped him with a wave of his hand.

Noah no longer had that much money, but he thought he remembered the payment rules of the governing authority. "Three hundred thousand. That's a tremendous sum. Please tell me how long I have to pay."

"Fifteen days," the man grunted. "Fifteen days. You either pay it by then, or we'll shut the project down and start selling what you have to pay the fine."

Noah looked at Japheth and then quickly thanked God for His precise timing and protection. "Fifteen days?" he said, looking up at the man. "Agreed. If you can come back in fifteen days, you can collect your fine."

The man stood up and looked arrogantly at Noah. "I'll be here," he said, as he turned and walked out.

CHAPTER 21

As the door slid open, Noah was overcome by what he saw and heard.

Ham was lying motionless in the bed. His eyes were barely open. His arms were resting on his stomach. The body recorders above him were brightly lit but strangely quiet. He looked much the same as he had for many days.

But Sicilee was there with him. She was gently, carefully washing his feet and applying oil to them. And she was singing to him. It was a soft, lovely, haunting song about God's love given to helpless, dying men. When she came to the last words — "When you don't know what to do, I'll still be there seeking you; if you'll just reach out your hand, I will take you to My land" — he felt his own face tighten with emotion and tears well up in his eyes.

When she had finished singing, she began to hum the song again. As he moved forward, she looked up at him, smiled, and continued to hum. She was still rubbing Ham's feet. Noah sat down across from her.

"Thank you, daughter," he whispered in her ear.

"You're welcome, father," she whispered back into his.

"How is he?" Noah asked in a hushed voice.

She frowned slightly. "I have hope, but . . . I don't know. He never smiles. I just wish he would smile, just once."

Noah took her chin in his hand and turned her face toward his. "If you keep serving and loving him that way, sooner or later a smile will have to come."

"I want to," she said, tears forming in her eyes.

"Tess was telling me that you're here every day. Your dedication has filled our hearts. I don't know what's moved you to do this, but I thank God for it."

She looked down at Ham. "Many years ago, there was someone who served me and loved me when my life was in a thousand broken pieces. I just want to do the same for others." She looked back at Noah, tears streaming down her face. "That someone was you," she said, with deep affection.

Noah put his hand on her face and brushed away some tears. "God only gives good gifts to those He loves. One of those good gifts He gave to me was you." He reached over and hugged her tenderly. "Thank you, my Father in heaven," he said softly.

"Thank you, my father on earth," she whispered to Noah. She smiled at him and, overwhelmed with emotion, looked down and began rubbing Ham's feet again.

"Has the doctor been here today?" he asked after several minutes of peaceful silence.

"He was just outside the room," she said quietly. "He said he'd be here in a few minutes."

They talked for several minutes about Nusheela. The pressure from Ham's illness had caused her to stay away from the family. Even though they were sure she had trusted God for her salvation, Noah and Sicilee were uncertain about her willingness to go with them on the box. They prayed for her for several minutes just before the doctor came in.

"I see the family's all coming together today," he said abruptly. "I just saw your wife in the hall, Seth-Lamech. I think I saw Ham's wife with her."

"Oh, good," Sicilee said as she stood up. "I'm glad Tess was able to get her to come."

The doctor examined Ham for about five minutes without saying a word. During that time, Tess and Nusheela came into the room and exchanged greetings with Noah and Sicilee.

The doctor made several entries into his small hand-held logicbox, watched the results, and then turned to face the family. "Not good," he said. "His health is deteriorating severely."

"What can we do?" Nusheela asked as she walked to Ham's side and put her hand on his face. "We must be able to do something."

"There's nothing more I can do here. I think there's another alternative before we get to light disintegration."

Noah, Tess, and Sicilee all reacted at the same time. "We'll *never* get to that alternative, doctor," Noah responded coldly. "We totally disagree with doing something to end someone's life."

"Oh, yes," the doctor said smugly. "The great Seth-Lamech and his opposition to light disintegration. How could I forget? Have you people ever seen some of the cases that get brought in here? Ending their lives is an act of mercy."

Tess was enraged. "How can you call that 'mercy'? Mercy is giving people *more* than what they deserve, not less. Mercy is serving and feeding and loving the helpless and the dying."

The doctor shrugged. "It's all a matter of how you look at it. Most people think that ending a valueless life *is* a greater mercy."

"Enough!" Nusheela said angrily. "Enough! We have to do something. Please tell me what it is."

The doctor handed her some records. "We'll have to send him to the healing center in New Eden."

"No!" Noah shouted, surprising everyone. "No!"

"Why not?" Nusheela asked, fear framing her face.

"Two reasons," Noah said in a lower voice. "First, I think they're doing things up there that could put Ham's life in danger. And second, think how *far away* he would be, and how *long* he'd be gone." He looked at each of the family members with a knowing expression. "I say no."

"I agree," Tess said quickly. "I think we should keep him here for at least another ten days."

"I say no too," Sicilee added.

"Well, I say yes," Nusheela said firmly. "I say yes. If he stays here, he'll die. How can we let him die? Didn't you just say that we have to do everything we can?"

"I did," Noah agreed. He stood up and went to her. "Nusheela, we all love him. I think any one of us would give our life for him. I know I would. He *does* need help. But what *is* help? Sending him away isn't help. He needs to be here when . . . when the time comes."

Nusheela backed away from him. "I don't know about that any-more! All I know is that my husband's dying, and there's help in New Eden. He has to go there!"

Tess walked over to Nusheela and took her hand. "Dear one, please listen to Noah. God will provide a way. I believe with all my heart that He'll heal my son—your husband."

Nusheela looked at Tess. "I'm grateful for your love. And I know that Noah is the one who brought my husband back. I'll never forget that. But I have to make my own decision now. What if I wait? Will it do me any good to bring a dead man onto the box?"

"Nusheela," Sicilee gently spoke to her, "I know that you trust Noah. You and I have shared in the past that we can trust him because he's a man of godly character, and because the whole intention of his heart is to serve God. Right now would be a good time to hold onto that trust."

"I'm not sure who to trust," Nusheela answered. "I . . . I'm just not sure. And just what are you trying to say?" Nusheela asked, with sur-prising antagonism in her voice.

Sicilee was very calm. "I'm just saying that you and I are both under Noah's authority. Your feelings are saying one thing and your authority is saying something else. Doesn't God want you to listen to the right voice—to Noah?"

"I don't know about authority anymore," Nusheela said weakly. "I don't know who to follow."

"Haven't you put yourself under Noah's spiritual authority?" Sicilee persisted. "Haven't you asked him to be your spiritual leader? It's easy to follow our leaders when they tell us easy things to do. Isn't this the time to listen to him—when it's the very hardest?"

Nusheela pulled away from Tess and glared at Sicilee. "Are you preaching to me? Who are you, to preach to me?"

The angry response surprised Sicilee. "I'm your friend," she said with hurt in her voice. "I just don't want you to make a mistake."

"*You* made the mistake!" Nusheela shouted. "You just want to keep him here for yourself! Why are you here every day? He's not your hus-band!"

Tess, standing behind Nusheela, reached out to take her arm. "Nusheela! You don't mean that!"

"I *do* mean that!" she exclaimed. "I don't understand why she spends all this time here. He's not her husband!"

"I understand her," Tess said from behind Nusheela. "She loves him very much, not in the romantic or lustful ways that you're thinking of. Not many people understand it, but a woman *can* love a man richly and deeply, even though she's not married to him, but with a pure and holy love. It's a special love that comes only from God."

Nusheela avoided looking at Tess and Sicilee. She looked instead at the doctor. "Doctor, I'm his wife. Who controls this decision?"

The doctor shook his head. "Nobody here but you. Your agreement is enough."

Nusheela walked around the bed to the doctor. "Then you have my agreement," she said strongly. "I want you to send my husband to New Eden. And I want you to do it today."

And then Nusheela, without looking at any of the others, left the room.

ها ها ها

In the area outside the room, Noah looked down at Tess, who appeared to be almost numb from the conversation with Nusheela. Noah went to her, stood in front of her, and lifted her face in both of his hands. "I love you," he said tenderly. "Very, very much."

"Noah, what are we going to do?" she asked frantically. "We can't leave him there, can we?"

"No, my dear one, no," he said reassuringly. "He's our son. We'll never leave him. No matter what," he heard himself saying with confidence, "we'll never leave him."

And as he kissed her, he prayed that God would keep his heart from melting.

CHAPTER 22

Noah and Tess were just finishing midday meal when they heard a loud knocking at the back door. As the door slid opened, Japheth and Sicilee almost ran into the room.

"Dad," Japheth said with emotion, "they've done it again."

"What have they done?" Noah asked as he took Japheth's hand and greeted Sicilee with a hug.

Sicilee put her hand on Noah's shoulder. "They've gone into the project and written their horrible blasphemies on the box again."

Noah visibly sagged. Sicilee hugged him again. "It's all right, Dad," she said encouragingly. "Their lies won't last much longer."

Japheth sat down. "It's like the box is a witness against them. They hate it."

Noah went to his seat, and all the others sat down. "Was there any other damage?" he asked, his voice seeming far away.

"Not much," Japheth responded, "except for the big hole they made in the back wall of the workspace. They did it right after dawn, as the first of our people were beginning to arrive. But the pack left just as suddenly. None of our people were even injured." Japheth poured a glass of juice and took a drink. "I can't explain it," he said as he put the glass back down. "It's like they were frightened off by something."

Tess touched Noah's hand. "Wasn't that when you were up, sitting on the bodyrest by the window praying?" she asked him.

Noah thought for a minute, then nodded. "It was. Praise God! I didn't know why I had awakened so suddenly. Now I know. It was God waking me up so I could be in prayer about this attack."

"Yes!" Tess agreed. "I know He'll continue do that kind of thing for us."

"He always has done that for me," Noah agreed, "especially when I'm walking very closely with Him. He'll make these things known to my spirit in an unseen but very real way." He looked around the table and smiled at each one. "He does that for me about the special people in my life as well—both in praying for you and for knowing when to contact you."

"I know He does that for you," Sicilee said tenderly. "There have been many times that I've thought, 'I really want to hear from Noah,' or I'll just be thinking about you, and you'll contact me. It's really special. Even before I answer, I usually know it's you."

Tess poured Sicilee a glass of juice. "God always does that for those who are one in spirit with Him and with each other. That kind of spiritual closeness is the heart of an intimate marriage or friendship. Noah and I have had that almost from the beginning of our relationship. And it's no secret that you two have that oneness of spirit."

"How's Shem?" Japheth asked.

The memory of holding Shem in his arms immediately came back to Noah. "What's it been, a week and a half, or two weeks?" he asked absently. "They really tried to finish him off. That life form was so . . . deadly. The doctors are amazed that he's still . . ." He stopped, unable to continue.

"The doctors are also amazed that your father didn't absorb the life form," Tess said quickly. "He held Shem so long, and . . . God was . . . gracious to them both."

Sicilee shifted in her chair. "I talked with Melena yesterday. As Shem seems to get sicker, her spirit just seems to sink lower and lower."

"That's understandable," Tess said sympathetically. "I'm dealing with those same feelings."

"God takes care of His own," Noah said, lost in thought. Then he sat straight up. "God takes care of His own!" he shouted as he slammed his fist on the table and caused a glass to spill.

"Noah!" Tess exclaimed as she quickly got out of the way of the flowing juice. Japheth started laughing, and soon the others joined in.

"I told you before I married you that he could be dramatic," Japheth said to Sicilee. "Once, when he was trying to explain something to us at a meal, he caught the edge of his plate with his hand." He winked at Noah. "Before then, I never knew that food could fly!" Everyone laughed again.

"Noah, please go on," Tess said as she finished wiping the table.

Noah rubbed his face. "What I was saying was that God takes care of His own. God hasn't forgotten any of us — including Shem. God just told me in the clearest of ways that . . . that all eight of us *are* going to get on the box! I don't know what God's got in mind, but I'm going to keep watching for Him to move." He paused, turning the glass of juice around and around in his hands. "In the meantime," he said softly, "*we* need to keep moving with our work."

"Dad," Japheth began cautiously, "that brings us back to the box. I know how you feel about the shaming of God's name, but I don't think we have enough time or people to get the project done as it is. You think we're less than ten days from the flood. Can we just ignore the . . . writing on the side? The box will be covered with water, and there won't be anyone left to see it."

"*God* will be there to see it," Noah said seriously. "And I'll know it's there. Our God is a God of order. If we do the right things first, the first things first, He'll honor our actions. We need to put a group to work on cleaning it up."

"I agree with your father," Tess said. "That box belongs to God, not us. It's a narrow passage into a new world, His way of taking care of His own. We can't let it be marked like that."

"I don't think I could get on it if it had that on the side," Sicilee said as she poured Tess more juice.

"All right," Japheth said with a smile. "All right. You all win. I'll get a group on it today. But Dad, there's another problem, too."

Noah seemed lost in his thoughts. "What?" he asked. "What was that?"

Japheth laughed. "Dad, it's always interesting watching you try to think about something and listen to a conversation at the same time."

Noah laughed in return. "They say our brain has two sides. Sometimes it seems like each of mine has a mind of its own!"

"Don't run yourself down," Tess chided. "Sometimes I think that half of your mind works better than all of mine." Everyone laughed. "Be careful," Tess continued. "I might think you're laughing in agreement."

"Never, Mom," Japheth disagreed. "You're the one who keeps this family running on a daily basis."

"I agree with Japheth," Noah said. "If I didn't have you . . ." He squeezed her hand.

Tess nodded with understanding. "Japheth, you'd better get back to what you were saying," she reminded her son.

"Dad, I don't know how it happened." He looked down at the table. "I was responsible for buying the pitch. I was sure we had enough. Now, this morning, Dainea tells me that we won't have enough to finish the last hundred and fifty cubits on the back side."

"Impossible!" Noah responded. "I checked it myself. There was more than enough."

"Could it have been stolen?" Sicilee asked.

"Why would anyone steal our *pitch?*" Tess asked.

Noah smiled at her. "Dear Tess, for the same reason that people would write blasphemies on the box. Sin. Plain, ordinary, black sin. They don't have to be able to use what they steal. All they want is to hurt us."

"I agree that it must have been stolen," Japheth said. "Maybe it was that pack this morning. The alarm was off to allow our people to come in. They could have had just enough time to take that much."

"So what are we going to do?" Sicilee asked.

"I only see one answer," Japheth said crisply. "We can't trust something so important to anyone other than Dad or me. Without pitch, I'm afraid the gopher wood in that section would . . . well, it could cause big problems."

Noah went to the fastcook and removed some cheese-covered bread. "I knew I left that in there too long," he muttered to himself. "Japheth, you're right of course. But you can't go. You're too important to the work here. The box is almost done, and it needs your attention. I have no design work or any other buying left. I'll take a small group in transports and get the pitch."

"I've already had Elimel place the order," Japheth said.

Tess, pouring water for Noah, added, "That poor man. He just hasn't been the same since . . . your father was attacked by that monster in his store. Elimel sometimes wants to talk about God, but he seems afraid to keep us in there very long."

"After that experience I don't really blame him," Noah said. "I paid for the damage and told him I didn't think it'd happen again, but he sees Nephilim behind every door."

"Maybe he'll join us," Tess said, her voice full of hope. "God could use that experience to draw Elimel closer to Himself."

"He could," Noah agreed. "Elimel's not hard like so many people are. I haven't talked with him for a while. I'll stop by to see him on my way out."

"It'll take you half a day each way," Japheth reminded him.

"Please be careful," Tess pleaded. "If anything happened to you, I don't think I could leave."

Noah stood up. "I've been in the palm of God's hand for six hundred years. I don't think He's going to stop protecting me now." He looked down at Tess's face, full of concern. "But I *will* be careful," he said, bending down to kiss her.

While Tess and Sicilee continued to talk, Noah went with Japheth to prepare the transports.

ॐ ॐ ॐ

"Our lives are over," Nusheela said emphatically.

Melena looked desperate. "I don't know, Nusheela. I just don't know. I . . . still have hope."

"Hope?" Nusheela exclaimed scornfully. "Hope? Ham's in New Eden, with the doctors giving him no real hope. And you can't even get near Shem in the isolation center. Melena, I almost can't stand to be around the others now and hear them talk about the box. How can you and I get on without our husbands?"

Melena visibly sagged. "Sicilee keeps telling me to expect God to do something special."

"Sicilee!" Nusheela said, irritated by hearing the name. "Sicilee! Why does she have so much interest in our husbands?"

Melena looked into Nusheela's eyes. "I heard what you said about her and Ham, Nusheela. But I think you're wrong. I really do think she loves Ham and Shem as a sister loves a brother."

"It seems like more than that to me."

Melena leaned forward and took Nusheela's hand. "Could it be that you're a little . . . well, a little jealous?"

"Jealous!" Nusheela responded, surprised. "Why would I be jealous of her?"

"Because you're really scared and confused and angry," Melena said gently.

After a long silence, Nusheela finally answered. "I . . . you may be right, Melena. I'm still not sure about Sicilee, but I *am* scared and confused and angry. I'm almost sick with fear. I've only been married such a short time, and now Ham's so . . ." She broke down into tears.

"I know," Melena said as she hugged her. "So is my Shem."

ð€° ð€° ð€°

"Stop the transport," Noah ordered the driver.

There in the pathway ahead was a crowd of people blocking the way. As they saw the transports come to a stop, the crowd began to walk toward them. Noah could see that they had signs. Some of the people appeared to be angry, while others were laughing. Noah was so close to home and yet so far away. He prayed for protection.

Now he could read the signs. Some had gross blasphemies, while others had personal insults about Noah and his family. The personal ones that hurt him the most were the ones describing him as a proud and arrogant man. He had been told that so often that at times it was hard not to believe it.

The large group stopped in front of his transport and formed a half-circle around it.

"Here's the great Noah Seth-Lamech!" one man near the front shouted. Noah recognized him as a former neighbor. He began shouting again. "Here's the man who has all the truth! The man who judges everyone! The man who builds ships where there's no water!" The man turned to face the crowd. "The man who should be in a mind treatment center!"

Everyone laughed and shouted in agreement. "More pitch!" a man standing near the second transport shouted. "More pitch for the great ship!" Everyone laughed again.

"You!" the first man shouted at Noah. "You're so hated by everyone that we can't even put our hatred into words. You with your preaching and your lies!" Several people threw books on the ground and the man set them on fire.

Noah stood up in the open transport. He could see that the books were copies of the one he had written. "I'll pray for you," he said, calmly but loudly enough for all to hear. Everyone laughed again.

"We'll pray for *you*," the man said mockingly. "You're the one who needs help. Do you know why? Because we want you to know what we intend to do. We're not going to stop you from building your foolish ship. But you'd better have a lot of food on it, because the day you go onto it, we're going to block you in and never let you out!"

This caused a new uproar, with everyone shouting different things. Noah stood up on the front of his transport. As he did, his heart sank.

Meta was standing near the front.

"Meta," Noah said sadly, "do you agree with this?"

"I do," Meta answered discourteously. "I think you're a madman. I'm sorry I helped you with your wicked work."

Noah was stunned by the words from this man. He had hoped for so much for Meta. But Noah knew he couldn't let himself be paralyzed by this personal discouragement. The serpent could have stirred Meta to come for just that very purpose.

Noah prayed, asking God to help him not to think about Meta's hatred, or to try to resist the serpent on his own. He asked God to clear his spirit, and to make him strong to answer this mob.

Suddenly Noah knew in his heart that the flood would come in exactly seven days. That the thought came at this particular time surprised him, and the shortness of the time overwhelmed him.

"People!" Noah shouted. "People!" The crowd quieted enough so that he could be heard. "I know you hate me. How I know that," he said with sorrow. "But that doesn't matter. The time is short! *My* judgment doesn't matter. But God's judgment does, and it's coming faster and sooner than you know!"

At that, people began to shout and curse. "We spit on your God," the man in front shouted at him. "We hate you and we hate Him. We wish He was here, so we could—" Noah blocked his ears to keep from hearing the terrible words.

Then Noah saw a sign describing Tess in despicable terms. Noah felt rage welling up inside. "Let me say one more thing," he shouted. The crowd quieted only a little. "I *am* going to get on that ship. And all of you can divide up everything else I own among you." At this, the crowd quieted even more.

"But this is my last thought for you," Noah continued, indignant. "May my God—the God of all that is, the God whom you will someday acknowledge as your Lord—swallow up those of you who refuse to repent. And may He do it while you stand on the very land that you so eagerly covet!"

The crowd was momentarily stunned. "Drive on," Noah commanded as he sat down, and the trembling driver immediately began to move. The shocked crowd parted quickly to get out of the way of the speeding transport.

CHAPTER 23

I t's hard to believe we're down to the last three days," Japheth said as he poked around his midday meal.

"I know what you mean," Noah agreed, looking through the window of the project office at the ship. "So much work, over so many years, and here we are — at the end."

"I went by to see Shem this morning," Japheth said, still chewing a bite of food. "They let me have ten minutes with him through the glass. It's not a very good way to talk, but they just won't let you in the room with him."

Noah stabbed at his food. "That's because the life form is so deadly. It's hard to keep up your faith when he looks weaker every day, Japheth, but somehow we've got to just hold on to God."

Japheth nodded. "Dad, I think he's still holding on to God. He was very sick this morning and could hardly speak. But when I held up three fingers, he knew what I meant. Three days left. He smiled and held up three fingers."

"Yes!" Noah exclaimed. "We have to keep believing, until we can get him out." He pushed his plate away and leaned back in his chair. "But I have to tell you, Japheth, I don't know how we ought to handle his situation. That life-form could spread to you just by touching him. I'm having second thoughts about letting you be the one to take him."

"Dad," Japheth said seriously, "you know I don't usually argue with you, but I'm the one to do it. I have my heart set on it. He and I have been counting down together. I want to be the one who tells him, 'this is the day, let's go.'"

"I'm still not sure," Noah said, almost to himself.

"Dad, I'm going to be wearing the protective clothing. And there really isn't any choice anyway. You have to be the one to get Ham from New Eden. I don't know my way around there at all compared to you."

"The timing on all this is incredible," Noah said as he looked up at Japheth. "It's well beyond even our most detailed plans. Without God watching us every step of the way, there's no way this can work out."

Japheth finished his meal and put his plate on the worktable. "I'm sure of that. I just don't—"

"There's a man here to see you," a voice said through the speaker on Noah's worktable. It was the guard at the front gate.

"Who is it?" Noah asked without moving.

"He says his name is Mizraim. Could it be the—" The guard stopped speaking for several seconds. "Yes, sir, it's *the* Mizraim."

"Is he alone?" Japheth asked.

"He has one man with him," the guard responded.

Noah looked at Japheth, who nodded his agreement. "Let them in," Noah ordered.

"I wonder what he wants here," Japheth asked with concern.

Noah shrugged his shoulders and sat back. "I don't know. He's been quiet for a while."

"Maybe he's repented," Japheth suggested.

"Now *that* would be a miracle!" Noah said. "That alone would make everything worthwhile."

"Seth-Lamech," the receiver said through the open door, "you have two visitors."

"Let them come in," Noah said to her.

She stepped aside and a huge, muscular man entered the room, looked around, and then turned and nodded to Mizraim, who was standing just outside the door.

"I can see you don't trust me," Noah said cheerfully. "I can't believe you consider me a threat."

"I don't," Mizraim bellowed as he came in and stood over Noah's worktable. "I've already told you that I consider you to be a dog."

"So much for repentance," Japheth said softly.

"What?" Mizraim demanded. "What did you say?"

Japheth sat up straight. "Before you came in, I was telling my father that maybe you'd repented and were coming with us."

Mizraim laughed. "Fools! You think someone like me would ever believe in your work? I came here to see if *you* want to repent."

"What?" Noah asked.

"I said I came here to see before I destroy your whole family, if you wanted to repent and give up this project."

"Why would we do that?" Japheth demanded.

"Why?" Mizraim walked over to Japheth and looked down at him. Noah was startled to see a large, new scar on Mizraim's face and neck. "Why?" Mizraim continued. "This thing has already cost you two of your brothers. They're both going to die. You and your father have both been beaten by the Nephilim. You can't even see out of one eye."

Japheth stood up to face Mizraim. As he stood up, the other man started to move toward him, but Mizraim stopped him with a wave of his hand. Even though Japheth was almost a cubit shorter than Mizraim, Japheth moved toward him until their faces were only half a cubit apart.

"I *can* only see with one eye," he agreed. "But I'd rather see what I see with only one eye, than to see what you see with both of yours."

Mizraim seemed very uncomfortable. He laughed and walked away from Japheth. "Your son has courage," he said, almost with admiration. "It's too bad that he's now deformed and worthless."

Noah stood up. "If being deformed means you're worthless, then you need to look at yourself in the reflector, Mizraim. It looks like someone did for you what you did for Japheth."

Mizraim's hand went instinctively for his neck. "Ah, I see," he said, dropping his hand and grinning at Noah. "You're talking about this little mark."

"Little mark!" Noah said. "That's no little mark, Mizraim. You're deformed. Does that mean—" All at once Noah knew what had happened. "Mizraim, it was a Nephilim, wasn't it? You brought them here to destroy my family, and now they've turned on you."

"I don't know what you're talking about," Mizraim growled. He glared momentarily at his protector. "Nothing can get to me."

"It *was* a Nephilim!" Noah insisted. "Yes! You bring them here and they turn on you. Your world is falling apart, Mizraim. Can't you see that? This is the time to turn to God, before you die in your sins."

Mizraim laughed. "I'm not the one who's going to die," he said menacingly. He pointed at Japheth. "But it's a shame that he has to die."

"What?" Noah asked as he stood up. "What are you talking about? Are you threatening my son?"

Mizraim sat down across the room. "I'm threatening all of you," he said, almost happily.

"Then please make your threat and leave," Noah said with disgust as he sat back down. "I don't have time for your games."

Mizraim's laugh was hideous. "But you *will* have time for my games! You fool! Several of my men have planted an explosive on your—what do you call it? 'The box'? They planted something on the box that's going to send you all to the pit—right after you get on."

"And when is that?" Noah asked.

"Three days," Mizraim responded. He smiled as he saw both Noah and Japheth react to his comment. "I have it right, don't I? In three days you're going to get on that thing and close the door, and then you'll have to wait—not knowing exactly when your lives are coming to an end." He laughed again.

"You're lying!" Japheth said angrily.

"No, son," Noah said quietly. "He's not lying. When this man promises violence, he always keeps his promise."

"Your father understands me!" Mizraim said with a sinister smile. "There *is* an explosive. You've been promising judgment for me and the rest of the region—the rest of the world. And now here I am to promise judgment to you! Ha! Now *you* have to repent and give up this project, because if you don't you're going to die!"

"We'll find it," Japheth said with uncertainty in his voice.

"You don't believe that," Mizraim said with disdain. "On a ship of that size, with as much as you've stored on there, you'll never find it in just three days." He walked toward Noah and slammed his fist down on the worktable. "Now, how do you like my little game, fool?"

Noah, looking very tired, sat back in his chair and looked up at his tormentor. "I don't know how you know the three-day schedule," he said slowly, "but I'll tell you that you're right. We *are* going to get on that ship in three days. And right after we do, Mizraim, you'll be sorry that you aren't on it, too."

Mizraim began to pace. "This man is so — " He stopped pacing right next to Noah and began to curse him. Noah closed his eyes and began to pray. "Fool!" Mizraim screamed at him. "Don't you understand? In three days *you're* the one who's going to die!"

"We'll see, Mizraim," Noah said quietly as he opened his eyes. "We'll see in three days who will die and who will live. But I'll tell you this: I'd rather die on that ship while I'm obeying God, than to die on land while I'm spitting in His face."

Suddenly, without warning, Mizraim spit into Noah's face. "I spit in His face and I spit in yours!" Mizraim screamed. Noah reached for a cloth and began to wipe his face. He never even stood up.

Japheth, however, started to move, but Mizraim's protector walked toward him and smiled.

"Go ahead, fool!" Mizraim shouted at Japheth. "My big friend here would love to tear you to pieces." Japheth stopped. "Your son has courage, fool, but he also knows when courage stops and beatings begin." He walked over to Japheth. "You deserve to die like a man, fighting my friend here. But I think I'd rather have you wait and die with the fool."

"I'd rather die with him, too," Japheth said coolly.

Mizraim laughed again and walked to the door. "One more thing. Many people think they're going to steal from you when you're on that wooden absurdity. But they're wrong! I'm going to have it all! Doesn't that make you feel good, knowing you're leaving everything you own to me?"

"I'll gladly leave it to you," Noah said, standing up. "It belongs to your world. It's a world that I joyously leave behind. Those things have no place in the world that I'm going to. But let me tell you something, Mizraim — you won't enjoy them for long."

"You won't see me again," Mizraim said.

"You're wrong, Mizraim," Noah corrected him. "I'll see you at the judgment seat of God."

"I'll see you in hell!" Mizraim screamed. He turned and walked out the door.

Noah sat down. He found another clean cloth and began wiping his face.

"That dog!" Japheth said as he sat down. "I can't believe what an animal he is, to come in here and do . . . that."

Noah leaned forward. "He's gone, Japheth. I just hope he keeps his word and never comes to see us again."

Japheth frowned. "How did he know our schedule?"

"I don't know," Noah answered. "Only a few people know it. Maybe he has listening units in one of our homes."

Japheth sagged. "What are we going to do?"

Noah leaned back. "We're going to get on the box in three days and leave everything we own to Mizraim."

Japheth stood up and went to the window. "Dad, he's right. We'll never find that explosive in three days. We could look for a month and not find it."

"Then I suggest you get a group looking for it," Noah said matter-of-factly. "It has to be a select group—if word gets around that there's an explosive on the box, we'll lose all our workers."

"Can the wives help?" Japheth asked as he turned around.

"Yes. I don't think Nusheela will come, but the others could be a big help. And I'll contact Jalel to see if he can get out here with some people to look for the thing. If we find it, we'll need him to remove it anyway."

Japheth quickly left the room. Noah walked outside. It was a beautiful day. As he walked through the entryway of the box, he looked to his left and saw a huge group of workers applying the last of the pitch in the far corner. He knew there was another, even larger, group working in the same area of the box on the outside.

Thoughts raced through his mind. He thought first about the way God was able to use the wicked to serve the godly, and how these men were working long hours to finish a project that they all scorned, building something that provided the only way for Noah and his family to live. These people were in the box right now, but they wouldn't be in it at the right time.

And he thought how ironic it was to pay these men wages that they would never get to spend now that the time was so short. He had recently doubled their pay to keep them working on Dainea's incredible schedule. He had just enough money left to make that commitment.

Japheth had tried to convince him not to spend the time putting money aside to pay these wages, since the next payday would be after the flood.

"What's the point, Dad?" Japheth had asked. "They'll never collect those wages anyway."

"I understand your thoughts," Noah said gently. "But I'm not responsible for those things. I'm responsible to be a man of integrity. I'll take care of my part and let God take care of His. I'm not God. I have to keep doing the right thing each day. Besides, what if they repent, and God is gracious and doesn't send the flood? What would be said of me and my God if these men went to collect their wages, and there was nothing there?"

"Many would say you were wrong," Japheth had suggested. "And all of your work on this project would be wasted."

Noah had smiled. "I'd gladly take the criticism and count my work on this project as nothing, if there would be true repentance and revival of the spirits of many people."

Noah was shaken from his thoughts by the alarm sounding the meal break. He turned to see several people bringing food in on pushcarts. He had been providing midday meals to the workers for over six months in his hope of finding any way possible to reach these people for God.

As they came to the tables, Noah searched their faces. He tried to see something, anything, that would indicate a spirit with a question. He was encouraged that some of these men and women might still come with him.

And then a new thought came to him. Perhaps some of them wouldn't come onto the ship, but would still repent when the flood came! Perhaps some of them would remember Noah and his words and his integrity and his funny box, as they ran into the hills and mountains to escape, or as they watched the wooden ship rising on the raging waters.

He saw in his mind people running even to the door of the box and scratching to get in. He could almost hear them crying out for help, but all earthly help would be gone forever. And then he could see a few, at their moment of death, asking God for the life that was truly life.

They might not save their lives on this earth, he thought, *but they can still save their lives where it really counted, in Paradise with all who had ever called on the name of the Lord.*

Noah was shaken from his thoughts by the sounds of the workers getting into line. As was his custom, Noah walked to the table and picked up a serving instrument. He smiled at the first man in line, placed some food on his plate, and asked him about his family.

CHAPTER 24

They started coming in the night.

Noah and Japheth had decided to alternate sleeping times so that one of them could be there at the right time. They knew, given the great variety of animals, that they had to begin coming during the night or the early morning hours if they were all going to get into the ship on time.

Noah, Tess, Japheth, and Sicilee had talked about it all week. The realization had come upon all of them at once that this, after all the years of labor and struggle, would be the first and only visible sign from God that they had been right.

And the animals had begun to come on Japheth's and Sicilee's watch.

"Dad," they heard Sicilee's voice pouring into their bedroom. "They're coming—I can't believe it! It's just like you said!"

Noah and Tess hurried to the table and turned up the sound on the receiver. "Go on, Sicilee. Tell us what's happening," Noah encouraged. He could hardly contain his excitement.

"Dad, Mom, it's so . . . wonderful," she responded. "At first we heard a far-off sound, like flocks of birds. And it *was* flocks of birds! But the flocks aren't all the same kind of bird. They're all mixed together!"

"This is too much," Tess said as she sat down on the bed and threw herself back on it. "I love it! Amen!" She sat back up. "I love it!" she shouted as she flung her arm into the air.

"What was that, Dad?" Sicilee asked. "I couldn't hear what Mom was saying."

"She's saying she loves it," Noah, trembling with joy, shouted into the voice-sender. "Sicilee, *I* love it. We *both* love it. We . . . I don't even know what to say." He grabbed Tess by the hands and began swinging her around. "Hooray!" he shouted.

"Dad," Sicilee shouted, "I don't know what's going on there, but I think it's the same thing Japheth and I were doing just a few minutes ago."

Noah went back to the voice-sender. He was out of breath and laughing. "Sicilee," he panted, "how many are there?"

"Dad, you were right," she answered, laughing. "There's seven of each kind."

Noah looked at Tess and started laughing again. "I knew it, Tess! I knew from the Lord that there'd be seven — three pairs for the new beginning and one for sacrifice. Praise God!" He looked back toward the receiver. "Sicilee! How are you getting them into the cages?"

"Oh, Dad, it's just so perfect!" Sicilee exclaimed with joy. "They're just flying right into the upper cages. When the first one filled up, Japheth opened another and they started flying in there! They're coming so fast. Listen!" She held her voice-sender into the air.

Noah and Tess heard the tremendous screeching and squawking. "I didn't know they'd come so fast," Tess said with glee.

"I didn't either," Noah agreed, smiling broadly. "Sicilee! Can you tell anything about which ones have already come?"

"No, Dad," she responded. "The only thing I know for sure is that the first one was a dove. I don't even know what some of these birds are."

Tess put her arm around Noah. "God is so good," she said. "He's bringing them from all parts of the world. Sweetheart, this proves it! It proves you were right all along. I'm sorry I ever doubted you."

He smiled at her. "You weren't the only one. I'm sorry *I* ever doubted God." He turned the sound level up again so he could hear the exquisite sound of a promise fulfilled. "Sicilee, can you at least tell how many there are?"

"I know we all thought they'd come slowly enough that we could identify and count them," she answered. "But there's no way. Japheth's already given up. We'll just have to trust God's count!"

"Yes!" Noah shouted. "We'll be right out."

"See you soon!" Sicilee said joyously before ending the contact.

Noah hugged Tess. "This is too perfect for words. We've got to get out there. We may not get much sleep these next few days! Yes!" He raised his fist in the air. "Yes!"

Tess rejoiced as she watched him try to calm down enough to get dressed. She hadn't seen him so excited in a long time. "There really isn't anything quite like a promise from God displayed before your eyes, is there?" she asked.

"No. Nothing! Amen!" he said, struggling with his clothes. He finally got his bodysuit on. "Tess, please call Melena while I finish getting ready. Tell her to come and see for herself, and then she can go share the good news with Shem. Make sure she has her protectors come with her. Then while you get ready, I'll see if I can get Nusheela to come. I think this would be a big encouragement to her."

They made their calls. Melena said she would come, but Nusheela was noncommittal in spite of Noah's best efforts. Noah and Tess went downstairs and got into the transport. As they raced along the pathway, Noah could imagine the stream of birds, flying at tremendous speed, filling up cages almost as fast as Japheth could open them.

"This could be the answer," he said enthusiastically. "Tess, how can those workers see this and not believe? This could be the answer."

"I hope you're right," she answered with joy. "I still can't believe it's really happening."

As they turned east off the main pathway onto the private pathway leading to the project, Noah sensed something—an intensity in the air. It was as though a fierce spiritual battle was raging all around them in the heavens. He looked at Tess, who was nodding. "I feel it, too," she said with awe.

As they came over the hill, they could see —a stream of birds, flying in a pattern that curved from the sky right into the door of the ship. They both shouted with great joy. Noah stopped the transport and they watched silently together.

"Tess," Noah said finally, his voice full of emotion, "it's just like when God brought the animals to Adam so he could name them. Here we are, you and I, for some reason chosen by God to be the start of a new earth, with animals brought to us by God. It's too . . . it's just too . . ."

"I know," she said, taking his hand.

"I'm just a man," he said. "Why would God do this for me?"

She reached up and turned his face toward hers. "It's because you fear Him and love Him, and because you've humbled yourself before Him. You've walked with Him, just like Enoch did. God took Enoch from this earth. And now He's doing the same for you."

Noah couldn't speak. He drove down the hill only to find the pathway through the gate filling up with animals of every kind—all running at a steady pace. "Look at them!" he shouted. "So many! I didn't know they'd be running when they came. Amen!"

Tess was pointing at the gate. "Look how they avoid hitting each other! It's like there are angelic shepherds protecting them and leading them in."

Noah slowly drove the transport to the gate. As they went through, the stream of animals continued around them. The animals never hit each other or the transport. "It's as if each one's on a rope leading it right into the box," Noah said. "I've thought about this a thousand times, but it's so far beyond my imagination."

"Look at the guard!" Tess shouted, laughing.

Noah leaned over and saw the guard standing in the gatehouse. The man was frozen into position and was staring at a fixed point in the line of animals. "Tess, I'm getting out," Noah exclaimed.

He jumped out of the transport and ran around to the gatehouse. "Hello," he shouted at the man but got no response. He went into the gatehouse and touched the man on the shoulder. The man didn't even move. Noah finally clapped his hands in front of the man's face, and he turned and looked at Noah. Fear filled the man's eyes as he slumped into a chair.

"What do you think?" Noah asked enthusiastically.

"I . . . I just . . ." The man shook his head violently as if he were trying to wake up. "What . . . what is it?" he asked.

"It's God," Noah said as he slammed his fist into his other hand. "God's bringing every kind of animal on the earth. And He's going to fill up 'Noah's folly' with them!"

The man looked up at him and then back at the line of animals. When Noah realized the man was unable to speak or listen, he ran out of the gatehouse and got in with Tess.

"What did he say?" Tess asked.

Noah laughed. "All he could say was 'What is it?'"

"What did you tell him?"

Noah squeezed her hand. "I told him it's God."

He stopped the transport and got out to open an additional gate. "I don't want the workers using the main gate," he explained to Tess as he got back in. "They might not be so careful with the animals." He drove the transport to the main door of the ship. "I can't wait to see the looks on the workers' faces when they get here!"

They walked up the ramp into the ship and through the entryway. Japheth was to their right, almost ready to close a cage full of camels and several other animals similar to camels in appearance. The open cage above it was filling up with birds. Sicilee was at their far left, almost too far away to see, just opening a new cage for some strange looking creatures.

"What are *those* things?" Tess asked, pointing and laughing. One animal looked like a pinecone with legs and a tail. Another one with a hard shell shaped differently from a turtle's looked ridiculous as it ran along on its short legs.

"I think . . . I think I don't know!" Noah responded gleefully. "I think I've seen images of some of them, but I don't remember their names."

Tess hugged him. "I think it proves that God has a sense of humor. You can almost see Him saying, 'Well, I think I'll put a tail right there.' or 'Let's see what this one'll look like with a long nose.' I love it!"

"I love it, too," Noah said. "Tess, you go to Sicilee. *I* want to see the look on Japheth's face."

Noah ran to Japheth. Japheth saw him coming and ran into his arms; they laughed and jumped up and down together until they both fell down.

"We'd better not stay on the ground," Japheth shouted with glee. "We're not to the biggest animals yet, but even the smaller ones are running so fast!"

Noah got up and looked into several of the huge cages. "I'm glad we made this level a full twelve cubits high," he said. He jumped into the air and shouted. He looked back at the door of the ship at the animals running through. "Japheth, I feel like a little boy again," he said with deep satisfaction. "This is an unbelievable statement from God to us!"

Japheth came to him and hugged him again. "I always believed you, Dad. But this . . ." he said with tears. After a moment he turned to see the open cage almost full. He went to it, closed the door, locked it, and went to the next cage. "They're separating themselves," he said, pointing at several full cages.

"I think it's God," Noah said. "He's the one who called them, and He's the one who's separating them."

"And He's calling the young ones," Japheth agreed. "The animals are mature but very young. There should be plenty of room—even for behemoth." They caught each other's eyes and laughed. "When do you suppose God will bring them?" Japheth asked.

"Knowing God," Noah answered with a smile, "it'll be after the workers go home tonight. We need their labor today and tomorrow. If they saw behemoth running through that gate . . ." Noah caught Japheth's eyes again, and they both started laughing uproariously.

"Behemoth!" Japheth shouted. "I want to be here to see that!"

"I do, too," Noah agreed. "Japheth, I want to go see Tess and Sicilee." Japheth nodded and Noah went to the other end of the ship where the two women were talking, and laughing at what appeared to be a very large rodent.

"Looks like God isn't forgetting anything," Noah said happily as he walked up behind them.

Sicilee turned and hugged him tightly. "It's too . . . wonderful!" she said, laughing. "This is the greatest thing I've ever seen!"

"Noah, look at this," Tess said. He turned to see her pointing at an animal with several large insects on its back.

Noah sat down on the ground and shook his head in wonder. "Even insects!" he said softly. "It's a complete creation, Tess. Nothing gets left behind. Not even insects."

And the three of them laughed until they cried from the awesome simplicity of what they were seeing.

ǝ ǝ ǝ

"Such a beautiful dawn," Tess said, exhausted, as she leaned against the side of the door. She was careful to stay far from the relentless surge of animals.

"Look at that," Noah, standing behind her, said in a whisper. "No line, except for a few hundred cubits on the other side of the gate."

The animals, coming from different directions, converged on the gate with perfect timing. The line never got longer or shorter, and the number of animals in line at any time seemed to vary with their size.

"The numbers are so great," Tess said above the noise. "How will we ever feed and care for so many?"

"I don't know," Noah admitted. "Some of these workers may still repent and get on here with us. If they don't—if it's just our family—I don't have any idea how we can care for so many." He held her close to his side. "But God wouldn't bring them if He didn't have a way."

☙ ☙ ☙

"You should've seen his face," Melena said as she sat down. "He's so sick, but he understood what I was saying. Oh, Dad, the doctors say they have no hope, but I'm glad that we do, and that Shem does."

Noah nodded in agreement. "When I was there two days ago, the most encouraging person in the whole place was Shem."

"When I told him about the animals," Melena said, "he held up his arm. I knew he was praising God."

Noah looked around the temporary table that he had set up on the first level of the ship. Tess had just brought a late midday meal and Sicilee had just sat down, exhausted, before Melena arrived.

"I knew he'd be pleased," Tess said. "This ought to give him even more hope."

"He's a strong man," Sicilee encouraged Melena.

Melena took a plate from Tess. "I agree. Please keep praying for him. Part of what he's fighting against is the discouragement from not being out here helping to finish the project. He doesn't say much about it, but I know he feels left out."

"That's just like him," Tess said as she sat down. "He always wanted to be part of everything we did as a family."

Melena stared at the full cages behind Noah. "I don't want to be discouraging, in the middle of all this joy, but do we know how we're going to take care of so many animals?"

"Noah and I were talking about that early this morning," Tess answered. "We were hoping that some of these workers would still repent and decide to come, but . . ."

Noah looked over at Japheth. He was directing some men who were working with the steady stream of animals coming through the door. Noah shook his head. "I still can't believe that some of them won't believe. I watched them as they came in this morning. They were so struck by the sight that some of them couldn't even get out of their transports."

Tess handed Noah a plate of food. "I have great hope for Dainea, though," she said encouragingly.

"I agree, Tess," Noah said. "She's always been interested in God. This could be the thing that convinces her. Jalel saw the animals as he came in, too. He's up on the second level looking for Mizraim's 'present.' I'm going to go up a little later and talk with him about the miracle of the animals."

"What about that time-planner you were telling us about?"

Noah shook his head. "He laughed when I first told him about them several weeks ago. I thought this would convince him, but when he saw the animals, he turned his transport around and left the site."

Melena frowned. "I hope we're all still thinking about how to convince Nusheela. She's very bitter."

"When the time comes," Noah said as he poured drinks for the others, "I think you three will be very persuasive. In fact, let's pray about that right now." They all bowed their heads. "Lord," Noah prayed, "please help these three precious women to convince our Nusheela at the right time to come with us. Even now, please prepare her heart so their words will find fertile ground." The others added their agreement.

"While we're speaking of fertile ground," Tess said, "I've always thought it was interesting that God chose us, a family involved in business, to begin again in a new world as farmers."

Noah nodded in agreement. "I've been reading a lot about it. You'll see, Tess. I'm going to plant a vineyard, and with God's help, we'll have fresh juice in a year or two . . . or three." They all laughed. "I suppose I don't know very much about it," he admitted, "but we'll learn together."

"How is Ham?" Sicilee asked. "Have we heard a recent report?"

"Yesterday," Tess answered. "They said they were going to do some major work on him on the eighteenth."

"The *eighteenth?*" Sicilee said, her face beaming. "Why, that's a day after we'll be —" She stopped.

"Gone," Noah finished. "That's a day after we'll be gone."

CHAPTER 25

S hem was dead.
Noah could hear Tess crying in the other room. He seemed frozen
to the side of the bed. He felt overwhelming grief and tears coming up
from the center of his heart.

He kept asking himself the same questions over and over again.
*How could Shem be dead? Where are you, God? How can I get on that
thing without my son?* Over and over, the pain of loss ripped through his
spirit.

He looked up at the wall. There, among many pictures, was a picture of Shem when he was ten. Noah wanted to get up, take the picture
in his hands, and hold it close to his heart. He tried to get up, but he
couldn't. He tried to reach for the picture. He stretched out his arm but
couldn't quite touch it.

Tess's crying grew louder. "No," he cried, burying his face in his
hands. "Please, God," he tried to pray, "don't let my boy be dead." As
he looked up again at the wall, the picture fell. As he jumped up and
reached to catch it, he began to fall.

"Oohhhh," Noah groaned as he suddenly sat straight up in bed.

He didn't know where he was. His clothing was drenched with
sweat, and he couldn't focus on anything in the dark room. He felt great
fear, almost panic. He threw off the covers and jumped up, but he felt so
dizzy that he had to sit down on the edge of the bed.

Suddenly, he realized that he couldn't hear Tess crying anymore. He
reached across the bed and was surprised to find her sleeping. He turned
his head quickly to look at the picture of Shem.

It was still there.

Finally, he began to realize that it had been a dream. Only it wasn't just a dream; he knew it was another attack from the serpent to discourage him and make him fear things other than God. This was the third morning in a row that he had awakened early after a massive spiritual attack.

"My boy is *still* alive!" he said, not too loudly, as he slammed his fist onto the bed.

Tess turned over. "What . . . what is it?"

"The serpent," Noah whispered to her. "Just the serpent. Try to go back to sleep."

"The . . . serpent?" she asked, only half awake. "What?"

"Nothing, dear," he said as he patted her arm. "Go back to sleep."

He got up quietly and dressed in the dark. As he walked into the hallway, he looked at the year-marker and stopped. It was the sixteenth day of the second month, 1656 A.C.. He looked at the next day and smiled as he saw that Tess had drawn a little picture of the ship in the open space.

He walked to the food preparation area and began to make himself something to eat. *Water this time but fire next time,* he thought, as he poured a drink of nectar. He sat down and began to eat.

He had asked himself many times why God had chosen water for this outpouring of His wrath. He had remembered the ancient teaching that the world was made by God from water and by water, and so it had finally made sense to him that God would use water to flood and destroy the earth.

Water to wash away the violence and corruption that so grieved God, he thought. *Water to cleanse the earth of its guilty conscience so that man could make a new start.*

And fire next time, he thought as he stood up and cleaned his plate and glass. He had often thought about the fire of the second outpouring of wrath prophesied by Adam. Noah had concluded that the far-off fire wouldn't just cleanse the earth, but would destroy it and make way for something brand new — something without the stench of sin and death.

As he wrote a note of love to Tess, a new question came into his mind. *How long will it be until the fire?* He knew that he would never know, at least while *he* was still alive on the earth. Other men, many years from now, would have to prepare their spirits for that judgment.

And then he stopped writing as a new thought startled him and took his breath away.

His own family! If only he and his family got on the ship, then the sin that would bring God's final judgment would come from his own descendants. The thought was so staggering that he had to sit down.

He saw clearly what he hadn't seen before — this judgment of water wouldn't bring the end of sin. He and his family were still sinners, and they were taking their heritage of sin and death with them. He understood now why they had to take the extra animals for sacrifice. God would take another action on another day to finally bring an end to the curse men had brought on themselves.

As Noah got into his transport and headed toward Methusaleh's home, he grieved that from his own home would come sin great enough to bring the wrath of fire. He hoped that his descendants wouldn't be as evil as the people he was leaving. And he purposed in his heart that he would work with his children's families for as long as he had breath to postpone that day of fire as long as possible.

ð ð ð

Melena and Sicilee stood side by side, arms around each other's waist, as they looked through the window at Shem, lying in bed with his back toward them.

"I hope he turns over so he can see us," Melena whispered. "It's only one more day before we leave. I want so very much to give him our encouragement."

Sicilee nodded. "Let's pray about it. *We* can't turn him over, but God can." She squeezed Melena's side. "You pray and I'll agree."

"Dear God," Melena prayed in a childlike voice, "please let my husband turn over. He's so sick, but we have an encouragement that should really help his spirit. You know we have to go to the box to work. Please, Father."

When they opened their eyes, they saw no change.

"Keep believing," Sicilee encouraged, as she held Melena even tighter.

And as they watched, Shem began to turn.

As he turned, his eyes caught the beautiful sight of two women he loved, smiling and then laughing, as they each held one finger high into the air.

ɜ ɜ ɜ

"Can't you see he's dying," Kenan said sharply. "Why don't you leave him alone?"

Noah sat down on the bed very near Methusaleh's head. "Grandfather, can you understand what I'm saying? There's still time for you to come with us."

"Leave him alone!" Naamah screamed. "You have no right to torment him like this. I hate you!"

"You're a terrible man," Kenan said. "I can't believe you'd keep bothering an old man on his deathbed. When will you leave him alone? The day after tomorrow, when your folly's clear even to you? When will you stop tormenting him?"

Noah looked at them. "You're the ones tormenting him, with your screaming and hatred. Why can't you—" He was stopped by a hand on his neck.

Methusaleh was pulling Noah's face close to his. With his other hand he was waving Naamah and Kenan out of the room.

"We'll go," Naamah said bitterly. "But I'll tell you this, Noah. The day after tomorrow I'm coming to your project so I can laugh at you as you come off that ship!"

"I'll be there with her," Kenan agreed. "I can't wait to see your face."

"You *won't* be there," Noah said sadly. "And you'll never see my face again—not on this earth."

"Fool!" Naamah shouted at him, as she and Kenan left the room. Noah felt sick as he realized he would never see his sister again.

"Noah," Methusaleh said in a faint voice. "Come closer."

Noah put his left ear by Methusaleh's mouth. "I can hear you," Noah said gently.

"Noah, Noah," Methusaleh said, barely able to breathe. "You're a good man. I don't know if you're right about this judgment, but I know you're a good man."

"Grandfather," Noah pleaded, "this is the last day to change your mind and come. Tomorrow is the day. Please come with us."

"Noah," his grandfather said, coughing, "I love you. But I don't think I'm coming with you. I'm . . . I'm not sure I'll still even be alive when tomorrow comes. I'm so . . . so . . ." He began coughing severely.

"But Grandfather," Noah protested, "you know that—" He was stopped by Methusaleh shaking his head and pulling Noah close to him again.

"Noah, I'm not coming with you," he said, almost convulsing. He took a moment to settle down. "Grandson," he finally continued, "I'm not coming with you. But pray for me. Pray for me this day and into the night. Perhaps you'll see me in Paradise."

Noah buried his face into the bed and hugged the old man tightly. "I'll be there, Grandfather," he said with tears. "I hope you'll make the right decision about God. And I hope you'll be waiting for me in Paradise."

*   *   *

"How's it going up here, Mother?" Japheth asked as he came into the common area on the third level of the ship.

"There's so much to do," she said, exhausted. "No matter how well you try to plan, there's always so much left to do at the end. If I had another week, I could find plenty to do."

Japheth hugged her and laughed. "I can remember when we'd take our family rests in the country. Dad would be at the front door shouting 'let's go' while you were still pulling the last things together. It's about the only time I ever remember your being a little frustrated with Dad."

She looked up at him and smiled. "Those were a little frustrating," she agreed. "He was always so aware of plans and times, and sometimes the plans wouldn't fit into the times!"

"The plan for this family rest makes those seem tiny by comparison," Japheth said, laughing. He suddenly became serious. "Such a long rest, Mom—with no going back."

Tess nodded and then walked a short distance to direct several people who were carrying a large table into the room. "Eight people, taking everything they need to start life over again. It takes my breath away."

"I'm having endday meal with Dainea," Japheth said hopefully. "We'll have ten, if we get Grandfather and Dainea to come."

"Yes. I wonder how your father's doing with Methusaleh."

Japheth shook his head. "His biggest problem is the time that Naamah and Kenan spend there. Sometimes I think that dying in the flood would be better than living with them."

"Japheth!" she admonished. "Don't even say such things!"

"I'm sorry," he said. "But even though they're family, they're not really family. Do you see what I mean?"

"I do," she said in a softer voice. "Yes, Japheth, I really do." She gave orders to several other men carrying chairs. "How's it going on the first level?"

Japheth whistled. "The animals are still coming. We still have about a third of the cages to fill, so I think that two-thirds of the animals must already be here."

"Your father would be proud of that statement of faith," Tess responded. "And how are . . . how is Jalel doing?"

Japheth looked very concerned. "Still nothing. The first level was easy, since it was largely empty when he checked it. But the second level, with all the boxes and supplies . . ."

"He knows his job," Tess said encouragingly. "More important, God knows our needs. He wouldn't bring us this far to let that monster Mizraim blow up the box."

Japheth hugged her. "I've got to get back to work," he said. "Let me know if you need help." As he walked away he shouted over his shoulder. "I'd still rather die on this ship than die out there with Mizraim."

"Me, too," Tess agreed, remembering Mizraim's advances against her in the city.

"Me, too," she said again, this time to herself.

ໄ ໄ ໄ

"I do see what you're saying, Japheth," Dainea said with affection. "It makes more sense every time we talk about it."

Japheth took a bite of bread. "Then, are you ready to give your heart to God?" he asked.

"That's a big step," she answered, looking around the common area on the third level. "A very big step."

"I know that, Dainea, but it's the only right step."

She nodded. "I *am* ready, Japheth. What do I have to do?"

"Just pray, Dainea," he said with growing excitement. "Just tell God you're sorry for your sins, you want to turn away from them completely, and you want Him to save you from sin and death."

Dainea prayed, a touching prayer that pierced Japheth's heart. As she finished he reached out and took her hand. "And now you can live, Dainea," he said joyously. "You can live forever with God, and you can get on this box with us."

"I agree!" she said softly. "I will get on, Japheth, if you'll let me."

"Let you!" he said, laughing. "Just try to stay off!" He looked into her eyes. "You've made God so happy, Dainea, and you've made me happy, too. I can't wait to tell the family."

"I know, Japheth," she said. "I can't wait either."

❦ ❦ ❦

"Tomorrow's the day, Elimel."

Elimel shifted uncomfortably in his chair. "What day?" he asked.

Noah sensed that Elimel was feigning ignorance. "You know what day, Elimel. The *last* day."

Elimel looked around his back room at the shelves full of goods. "The last day," he repeated absently. "The last day." Suddenly he focused on Noah. "How do you . . . *know?*"

Noah smiled. "I've told you many times about listening for the voice of God. God knows so much more than us, Elimel, but He tries so hard to tell us everything we need to know. The hard part is we don't like to listen."

"Are you saying I don't listen to God?"

"All I'm saying," Noah answered gently, "is that this is the most important night of your life for listening to God. Tomorrow, all of this will be gone. My hope is that you won't be swept away with it."

Elimel stood up and walked several steps away. "Noah, I think you're sincere, and that you really care about me. I don't know why, but I think you really do. But to leave all of this . . ."

"I know it seems hard," Noah pleaded, "but please make the right choice. Elimel, tomorrow is the *last day*. There won't be any more days to make decisions."

Elimel walked to Noah and patted his arm. "I'll think about it," he said. "If I decide to go, I'll be there in the morning."

Noah looked into the man's eyes. "There'll be room for you, Elimel," he said affectionately. "And a long celebration if you come."

ᴢᴀ ᴢᴀ ᴢᴀ

Noah looked at Japheth, crumpled up in an old bodyrest in the corner of the project office. "Son, I think we've both had three days since last night."

"I agree," Japheth said without moving. "But I wouldn't have missed this for anything. Watching those last animals come in was . . . unbelievable. I've never felt so close to God."

Noah leaned back in his seat. "Neither have I. Those large cold-blooded animals spoke to me of God's power and majesty."

Japheth sat up. "I've never seen a behemoth before, except in images. When they came, you could hear the other animals almost screaming in fear. You could almost hear *me* screaming in fear. I'm just glad God brought younger ones."

"From some of the images I've seen, the largest ones wouldn't fit into the cages. God gave us the overall dimensions of the ship, Japheth, and He made the animals. He knew perfectly which ones to bring."

"Should we go over the plans again?" Japheth asked as he stood up and came to Noah's worktable.

"Yes," Noah said, as he leaned forward and pulled some papers out of a pocket in his bodysuit. "I'm going to be in New Eden about two hours before dawn. I'll be at the healing center right before dawn. That should tie in well with your pulling Shem out of isolation about an hour later."

"Melena says that the workplan changes every day at that time. She's been watching it to make sure there are no changes."

Noah nodded. "Make sure you wear your—" He stopped, sensing something wrong. He suddenly felt that there was someone outside the office door. He pointed to the door, and Japheth got up and walked quietly to it. "Make sure you wear your protective clothing," Noah said in a normal voice. "We don't need you to—"

Japheth pushed the presspoint and the door slid open. He reached through it and pulled in a woman, who grunted as she came headlong through the door.

"Dainea!" Japheth said with surprise. "I thought you went home three hours ago." He looked at her hand. "What's that?" he asked suspiciously. And then he knew. "Dad! It's a recorder!"

"What?" Noah exclaimed. The whole truth hit him at once. "Dainea," he said, standing up, "are you the one who's been giving Mizraim our plans?"

"Yes, I am!" she shrieked at him. "I've told him about everything, every day!"

Japheth was crushed. He couldn't believe this was the woman who had prayed with him just a short time before. "Dainea," he pleaded, "I thought you were really interested in God."

"Fool!" she screamed at him. "I *hate* your insulting talk about your God who doesn't exist. Having to listen to you, I nearly choked on my meal."

Japheth was becoming angry. "Do you mean you'd work for us, help us, and then help that man put an explosive on here to kill—"

"Yes!" she shouted. "Yes! Mizraim is my *man*. We've lived together for five years. He hates you. I hate you. And you'll never find that explosive." She laughed and held the recorder up. "Even if you did, you'll never get on this ship. When I give this to Mizraim, he'll have commanders waiting for you at the isolation center."

Noah walked around his worktable. "There's one thing you're forgetting," he said to her in almost a whisper. "You're not going to take that recorder to Mizraim."

ta ta ta

Noah and Japheth sat down on the bodyrest across from Dainea. They had tied her securely and gagged her to stop her cursing. It had taken about thirty minutes because of her violent struggling and fighting.

"We're going to have to bring her, Dad," Japheth said, exhausted.

Noah shook his head with disgust. "We can't. We can't take anyone on this ship who doesn't belong to God. We'd find ourselves standing against God. We'd be rescuing her from God's wrath." He looked at her intently. "No, we'll just have to hold her here until we're ready to go."

"She could still change," Japheth said, discouraged. "I guess I just don't want to give up hope."

Noah shook his head sadly. "There's no room in God's plan to save those who *might* change after His deadline's passed. Her time to decide has already passed. But if you have any doubts, ask her. Ask her now."

Japheth stood up and walked to the woman. "I'm going to take this off your mouth," he said gently. "You've been listening to us. You've heard so much about God these last several months. Think before you speak. Do you want to come with us?"

When he removed the gag, she spit into his face. He jumped back, moaning with disgust. She cursed him bitterly, until Noah finally put the gag back into place.

ta ta ta

In the first hour of the last day, Noah walked across the workspace to the door of the huge shadow that was his ship.

Everyone had gone. He had decided on an impulse to walk through the ship one last time before the intensity of the next day absorbed his attention. As he walked through the door, he praised God for this slender passage into light.

He turned to his right and began walking down the first level. He looked into several of the cages and smiled as he remembered how God had brought these animals to him. Every cage had been filled; there were no empty spaces, and no cage was too full. Nothing in Noah's life, except for the ship itself, had ever so clearly spoken to him about God's perfect provision.

And then it came to him.

There wasn't a single sound coming from anywhere on the entire first level. There were thousands of animals, and not the smallest sound. He began walking quickly, reaching the end of the ship and walking down the side opposite the door. Every animal was asleep.

He didn't know what it meant. He knew there was no clear explanation for what he was observing. He told himself that this many animals couldn't be that quiet, certainly not for more than a few seconds. And yet here they were, minute after minute, almost as though they were dead.

Fear suddenly gripped Noah, a sickening fear that all of the animals *were* dead. He began to search frantically for signs of life — breathing, movement, anything. He thought of Mizraim and how he would delight in killing all of God's creatures. Noah grabbed a cage as he felt his legs giving way beneath him.

He closed his eyes and began to pray. "God, dear God," he said, weakly. "Please, no. No, dear God, no. Please don't let it be so. Please don't let these animals you've given to me be dead."

And then he heard it — ever so slight but clear. As his spirit quieted down he could hear the faint sounds of breathing. It wasn't normal breathing, but it was there. He opened his eyes and saw the dark outline of a black bear. As he peered through the darkness, he could see the animal's chest moving ever so lightly.

He went from cage to cage, stopping to listen and watch. After several minutes he finally stopped and lifted his hands in the air.

"Praise You, God!" he shouted. "I don't know what this is, I don't know what to call it, but I see what You've done! Praise You!" In his heart Noah knew that this was a special kind of sleep, designed by God for the long journey ahead. Somehow, he also knew that it was meant for the animals' care in the new world to come.

He went to the second level, so full of storage rooms and crates. Jalel had finally gone home, too exhausted to continue his search for the explosive. Noah walked along the corridors, pointing his quicklamp ahead of him and to the side, wondering if he had wisely spent his resources to bring the things that would count. "It's too late to think about that now," he said out loud.

About the second hour he made it to the third level. He walked past the huge storage rooms into the common area, so beautifully and warmly decorated by Tess. "Thank You for her, Lord," he said aloud. "We'll have many special times here, for as long as You keep us on this ship."

He looked around at the entrances off the common area leading to each family's living space. He decided to go into the area that had been designated for Tess and him. He went into the visiting area and smiled. He had teased her about all of the lovely images she had taken time to find and put on the walls. Standing there, thinking how long the journey might be, he was glad that she had persisted in her special work.

He went through the eating area into the back part of the living quarters. As he walked up to the door of the bedroom, he could see a note hanging there. He walked quickly to the door and smiled in anticipation.

"Dear one," it read, "I know in my heart that you'll be here tonight. I've known you long enough and well enough that I know you'll have to walk through this big funny box and think about everything one last time.

"The world we know is coming to an end, but it has one light—you, the only son of light. I don't know where we're going, and I don't know how long it'll take to get there, but I thank my God that I'm going there with you."

Noah went into the room and sat down on the bed. He leaned his head back and looked up through the window above him. The moon was shining high in the unending night, and its beautiful glow filled the room with soft light.

He looked up at the image of Tess that he had placed on the dressing table just a few cubits away. He smiled at the face that was smiling at him.

"And I with you," he said with quiet joy.

CHAPTER 26

They stood together in the rich greenery just a short distance from the healing center; it was still dark and cool. They could see several people going in the back entrance. The man looked down at his timekeep.

"It's almost the change of workplans," Noah said in a hushed voice. "We'll need to go in a few minutes. How are you doing?"

Sicilee moved closer to him. "I think I'm all right," she whispered. "I have to admit I'm frightened. I didn't sleep at all last night."

"I didn't either," he said as he looked through the plants behind him. He peered down the long hill to the pathway far below. "I told Tess yesterday that I need to sleep for a month. Maybe God will be gracious and allow that on the box."

"I spent the night praying about this," she said. "And about Japheth's work with Shem."

Noah hugged her. "I did, too. I think we can add our prayers to another's even if we're not together."

"I agree," she said. "Do you think we'll be able to get in there just at the right time between workplans?"

"I hope so," he said, fighting strong feelings of anxiety. "I think your part in this is so important, but I hate having to expose you to danger like this."

She squeezed his hand. "We've all been living in danger for a long time — you most of all. We have to take Ham with us. It's worth everything to try."

"I'm glad you think so," he said. "Let's take time for a short prayer, and then we'll have to go."

Sicilee prayed for God's protection on their effort. As soon as she finished, they moved from their hiding place onto the walkway leading to the back entrance. "I'm still fighting fear," Sicilee whispered.

Noah looked at her. "I am, too, Sicilee" he said. "I am, too."

*   *   *

"I *will* come, Tess," Kedrah said, "but I just need a little more time to . . . well, you know . . ."

Tess moved closer to her and took her hand. "Kedrah, dear, there *isn't* any more time. None. You have to decide now."

"I know that, Tess," Kedrah said, tears filling her eyes. "I know that. I just don't . . . I need more time . . ."

"Time for what?" Tess asked, a little sharply.

"Tess," Kedrah said, sniffling, "oh, Tess. I love Pelenah, but I really am coming, unless he kills me first. If I stayed, I'd feel so bad . . . I know I have to come."

"Then come with me *now*," Tess urged. "If you wait—if you think about it too long—you'll miss God's time. You'll be dead, Kedrah. I love you too much to want to see you dead. Please, dear friend, come with us."

"I want to, Tess," she said suddenly and she stood up. "Let's go."

Tess jumped up, smiling. "Oh, Kedrah, thank God! It's the right decision."

They walked hand in hand to where Kedrah had placed several clothesboxes. "I'm not sure I remembered everything," she said.

"It doesn't matter," Tess reassured her. "We have so much of everything. Just come, Kedrah. We have to hurry."

They picked up the clothesboxes and went outside into the darkness. Tess was so excited that she almost ran to the transport. She opened the door and began to put some things in, before realizing that Kedrah wasn't nearby. Tess turned around, but there was no one to be seen.

Tess ran back to the door of Kedrah's house. "Kedrah!" she shouted. "Kedrah! Are you in there?" She began pounding on the door.

"Go away, Tess!" Kedrah yelled from inside. "Please leave me alone. I just can't come right now. Maybe I'll come later."

Tess started to plead but realized that there was no point. "Kedrah, dear, I know you're confused," she said, trying to control her overwhelming discouragement, "but there's still time. Please come as soon as you can."

After a brief pause Kedrah shouted through the door. "I will, Tess. I'll come soon."

Tess walked slowly to her transport and got in. As she began to drive away from the house, she had to stop for several minutes to pray for strength, and to cry for Kedrah.

ﻬ　ﻬ　ﻬ

"I can't believe it," Melena whispered as they walked along the winding pathway toward the back of the isolation center. "It's the most beautiful dawn I can remember seeing."

"It *is* a lovely day," Japheth agreed. "Somehow I expected it to be . . . different."

Melena stopped and looked up at the sky. "I did, too. I thought the heavens would be full of warnings. I thought the earth itself would be crying out on its day of destruction."

"No warning," Japheth answered somberly. "No warning at all. We should have known. If they won't listen to truth, they won't listen to signs in the sky either."

Melena looked up at the imposing building towering in the distance. "I can't believe it, but it's true. They'll never know. Right up to the last minute, they'll never know."

Japheth stopped walking and looked into her eyes. "Are you sure you can do this?" he asked seriously. "You're so quiet and gentle, I have to say . . . well, are you sure?"

She nodded. "I am. With God's help I can do it." She smiled at him. "The acting I did at my training center should help."

He searched her eyes and then began walking again. "May God help us this next two hours."

"Amen," she answered.

ia ia ia

"You have to get control of yourself."

Tess was surprised at the strong words she had spoken. She had awakened Nusheela with a loud knock just as dawn was breaking. The time together since then had gone very poorly.

"I don't want to listen to this," Nusheela said angrily. "My life is ruined. My husband is dead. I have nothing to live for."

"Stop saying that!" Tess commanded. "Ham *isn't* dead! He's going to live. The only question I have is, are you going to live and join him on that ship?"

Nusheela began crying. "I can't get on that ship," she sobbed. "I don't know what's going to happen, but I can't get on that ship and leave my husband behind."

Tess went to her and sat down. "That's what I came here to tell you, Nusheela. You *won't* have to leave him behind."

"What?" Nusheela said, startled. "What do you mean?"

"Even now," Tess said slowly, "even now, Noah's getting ready to bring your husband back from New Eden."

"What? No!" Nusheela screamed as she stood up. "He can't do that! Ham will die. Ham will die. Ham will *die!*" She started to run toward the door, but Tess jumped up and stopped her. "Let me go!" Nusheela screamed. "I've got to stop him. Ham will die!" She cried and screamed uncontrollably.

Tess finally let go of her but held onto her shoulders. "Stop that, Nusheela!" she ordered. "Stop that!"

When she wouldn't stop, Tess slapped her hard in the face. Nusheela sagged to the floor, where she sat and continued to cry softly. Tess sat down next to her and put her arms around her.

"It's all right," Tess said as she rocked her gently. "It will be all right."

ia ia ia

"You look very interesting," Sicilee said to the man behind the worktable. "Would you be able to go to the eating area with me and talk for a few minutes?"

The man was the only person in that part of the building at this early hour of the morning. The healing workers from the earlier workplan had already left, and the workers about to come in were receiving their instructions for the day. Sicilee and Noah knew that they only had about fifteen minutes to save Ham's life.

"Uh, I don't think so," the man said with frustration. "I'd like to, but I could really get into trouble if I left right now. Maybe we could go a little later?"

Sicilee shook her head. "I don't think so. The reason I asked was that I don't want to be seen by all those people. We can talk and get to know each other."

"Fifteen minutes isn't much time," the man muttered. "If you want to —"

"Not *now*," she said, with a real toughness in her voice. "This would be a time just to talk. Other things will have to wait." She looked up and down the hall. "Hurry up," she insisted. "We don't have much time."

The man looked down at his desk and then back up at her. He also looked up and down the hall. "I shouldn't . . ."

She put her hand on his face. "Decide," she said softly. "What can happen here in fifteen minutes?"

He began to walk around the worktable. "Nothing," he said. "Nothing ever happens here." He put his arm around her and began walking down the hall. "Let's go," he said with anticipation.

🙨 🙨 🙨

"You're not doing anything for my husband," the woman screamed at the two men standing in front of her. "What kind of place is this? What's the matter with you people?"

The men seemed helpless to deal with her. "We're doing everything we —" one began.

"You're doing nothing!" Melena screamed, walking right up to him. "You people are fools!" She paced up and down, screaming at the top of her voice.

The other man finally walked up to her and grabbed her arm. "Woman, you don't have any right to talk to us this way."

"Pig!" she screamed as she pulled away. "Pig! Let go of me!"

"What are we going to do with her?" the first man asked as he looked fearfully in both directions.

"I don't know," the other man answered. "We can't let her go on like this. If the wrong person hears her, we could be in trouble."

"You *are* in trouble," she screamed. "My husband's in there dying, and all you can do is keep me away from him. Where's all your healing knowledge? Why can't you help him? Pigs!"

As she began to run toward the room where her husband lay dying, the second man ran after her and grabbed her. She struggled to pull away. "Help me!" he shouted at the other man. "She's too—get over here and help me!"

The other man hesitated but finally came over and grabbed her by the arm. She pulled and pushed and kicked, causing the second man to let go for a minute. "Grab her!" the other man commanded. "We've got to get her out of here!"

When they had finally gotten a secure grip on her, they dragged her down the hall. Japheth heard her scream and could see the big man hitting her in sensitive areas. He almost started to run after them but stopped when he remembered the plan they had agreed on and prayed about. Melena had told him not to alter the plan, not even if they killed her. He gritted his teeth as the screaming continued.

"Help her, God," he prayed against the choking fear. "Please help her now."

ð   ð   ð

"What have we got here?" the man said, surprised at the sight of a woman tied and gagged. "Why, it's Dainea!"

Jalel walked to where she was sitting and removed her gag. "Those animals!" she shouted, spitting to clear her mouth. "Untie me," she demanded, looking up into Jalel's large face.

"I'm not untying you," he said suspiciously, "until you tell me what's going on here."

"Those animals did this!" she screamed. "Get me out of here." She squirmed to try to release herself.

"It's no use," he said evenly. "Whoever did this knows how to make a knot."

She finally settled down and changed her expression. "Jalel," she said softly, "you know me. Noah and Japheth did this to me. They attacked me, and then they tied me up like this so I couldn't tell anyone."

Jalel looked at her in disbelief. "They what? They *attacked* you?"

"Yes," she said, nodding. "Last night, it was just the three of us here. Japheth grabbed me and took advantage of me. The whole time his father was watching and laughing."

Jalel sat down. "I can't believe it. Those two men seem so—"

"Those two men are just like all other men," she said. "Men all want the same thing. You think they're so holy, but they're animals. Only an animal would tie a woman up like this." She looked at him strangely. "Only an animal would *leave* a woman tied up like this. You're not an animal, are you, Jalel?"

Jalel was totally confused. "I guess I'll untie you," he said. "And then we'll go find Seth-Lamech and get this thing straightened out. I can't take too much time, since I've still got to find that explosive." He reached down with a cutter and removed the ropes.

"Thank you," she said as she stood up.

"Let's go," he said, turning to walk away.

As he took his first step, he felt a crushing blow on the back of his head. "You go . . . to the pit!" he heard her scream as he lost consciousness.

ᵕᵕ ᵕᵕ ᵕᵕ

Noah had waited until Sicilee and the man were out of sight. He knew he only had about ten minutes left to rescue his son.

The security was lax, as it seemed to be at all healing centers except those handling isolation cases. He went into the room where Ham had been since being brought here. "Help me, God," Noah prayed as he began to remove the elemental inserts from Ham's gaunt body. "Don't let me do anything to hurt him."

He moved quickly, feverishly. After removing the last of the inserts, he found Ham's bodysuit and began to dress him.

"What's . . . what's going on . . ." Ham said groggily as he tried to turn over.

"It's me, son," Noah said gently.

"What . . . are you . . . doing?" Ham asked, only half awake. The drugs had been effective — drugs to cause pain, drugs to stop pain — all had seemed to take away his mind.

"I'm taking you with me," Noah answered calmly. "Today's the day, son. Today's the day, and we're going to a new earth."

He looked down to see Ham crying.

"Oh, Dad," Ham said, confused and sobbing. "I can't believe it. I . . . prayed in . . . to . . . prayed about you, and this . . . oh, Dad, I prayed . . . to go. I want . . . to go."

Noah felt the sting of his own tears but smiled at his son's words. "I was praying, too," he said in a hushed voice. "I was praying that you'd want to come."

"I do . . . Dad," Ham said, straining to sit up. "I asked . . . God to . . . forgive me and . . . I want . . . to . . . come." He fell back onto the bed, exhausted, but smiling.

Noah stopped and quickly praised God for this great miracle. Then Noah finished dressing him and helped him to sit up. "Ham, I'm going to pick you up and put you over my shoulder," he said, holding Ham's face in his hands and looking directly into his eyes. "I'll try to carry you carefully, but I have to move fast. Please try not to make any noise." Ham nodded in agreement but could say nothing.

Noah stood up, praying for strength to carry his son. He bent down and kissed him on the cheek, and then whispered "I love you" into Ham's ear. He smiled as he heard a subdued "I love you . . . too," from his dying son.

Noah picked up the trembling body and lifted him over his shoulder. He grabbed Ham's legs firmly and turned toward the door. "Pray, son," he said. "If anyone sees us, we're through. Pray that God will blind their eyes."

They made it to the innerlift and down to the first level without seeing anyone. As Noah, half walking and half running, staggering under the load, got to a point just fifty cubits from the back entrance, he saw a large healing officer walking toward him. Noah stopped and waited for the confrontation.

The man walked by, never once looking at them.

Moments later, in the place where Noah and Sicilee had prayed for success, Noah laid his son down on the ground. Breathing heavily, Noah sat down next to him.

"What . . . what are you . . . we waiting for?" Ham asked, one eye closed and the other only partly open.

"A woman," Noah said breathlessly. "A woman who loves you very much."

He looked down to see Ham's open eye searching Noah's face. "Nusheela?" he asked. Noah shook his head. "Sicilee?" Ham asked.

"Yes, son," Noah answered. "Sicilee. May our God bring her to us soon."

"Amen," Ham murmured.

🙥 🙥 🙥

The sick man looked up at a man dressed in a white protective bodysuit. "Who are you?" he asked weakly.

"I'm the one who's going to take you home," the other man said, his voice sounding eerie through the speaker in the headpiece.

Shem tried to sit up. "Who?" he asked, confused. "Who?"

"It's Japheth," he answered. "Today's the day, brother. We're going home."

Shem, smiling, fell back onto the bed. "Yes!" he shouted victoriously. "I knew when I saw Melena and Sicilee yesterday that the day was almost here. Yes!"

Japheth sat down on the bed. "It *is* here, brother. Praise God, it *is* here."

Shem touched Japheth's arm. "Thank you for saving me, Japheth," he said with affection. "May my descendants someday save yours."

"I've got to get started," Japheth said, embarrassed. "We haven't got much time." He pulled some clothes out of a bag he had brought with him and began to dress Shem. "Will you be able to walk?" he asked.

Shem nodded. "I think so. They haven't let me move around very much. But this day I think I'll be able to make it—at least for a while."

"Good," Japheth said, as he finished dressing him.

"How are we going to get out of here without being seen?" Shem asked, concerned.

"Right now, there's no one out there," Japheth answered cautiously.

Shem looked sternly at his brother. "There's *always* someone out there."

"Not today," Japheth answered as he stood up. "We've got to go."

Shem stared at Japheth. "How do you . . . how did you get that to happen?" When Japheth didn't answer, fear gripped Shem. "Is it Melena? Is Melena doing something to get those men away from here?"

Japheth nodded. "She found a way, brother. As we go, we'll pray for her."

"I won't go," Shem said firmly. "If she's still here, with men like those—I won't go."

Japheth grabbed his arm and pulled him up. "You *have* to go!" he said, almost angrily. "You have to go. That lovely young woman has risked her life this morning to get you out of here. Are you going to waste that? Let's get out of here!"

When Shem hesitated, Japheth took his arm and pulled him toward the door. Shem resisted at first, but finally began moving on his own. "What have they done to her, Japheth?" he asked, overwhelmed.

Japheth felt his own emotions welling up. "They hurt her," he admitted, tears filling his eyes as he remembered the beating. "She's a special woman, brother. A woman of faith. I hope you always treasure her."

Shem nodded. "I will," he answered. "I just hope I get to tell her so."

"You will," Japheth said confidently, as he put Shem's arm around his shoulder and led him through the door.

❧ ❧ ❧

"It's time to go," Tess said to Nusheela. "We want to be there when the rest of them come."

Nusheela's face was streaked with tears. "Tess, I'm so . . . I don't know what to say."

Tess took her face in her hands. "You've been through a lot."

"No excuses," Nusheela said, sniffing. "I've been so far away from God . . . and from you. I've let anger and bitterness swallow me up. In my heart I blamed you and Noah for what happened to my husband. I hated that ship. And now . . ." She wiped her face with her sleeve. "Oh, Tess," she cried, reaching over to hug her, "will you forgive me?"

"Yes, dear, yes," Tess said tenderly, as she hugged her. "I forgive you."

"Do you think Sicilee will ever forgive me?" Nusheela whispered in Tess's ear.

"Yes, dear, yes," Tess answered. "We'll pray in the transport. But right now, we have to go."

The two women got to their feet. "Is there anything else you need to bring?" Tess asked. "Any other prized possessions here?"

Nusheela looked around the room and then into Tess's eyes. "Nothing here," she said, smiling victoriously. "All of my prized possessions — all seven of them — are going to be with me on that strange, funny, wonderful ship."

Tess hugged her tightly. "How unusual," she said joyously into Nusheela's ear. "I have exactly seven, too."

CHAPTER 27

"S omeone's coming!" Nusheela, standing at the top of the ramp, shouted. "I think it's Japheth's transport!"

Tess came to the door and stood at her side. She squinted at the transport coming down the distant hill. "I think you're right," she said. "It does look like Japheth."

They watched together as the transport sped toward the gate. The project site was strangely quiet; Noah had paid the workers for the day and told them not to come. As far as Tess and Nusheela knew, they were the only two inside the fenced area.

As the transport came up to the ramp and stopped, they watched with joy as Japheth jumped out and began waving at them. "Help!" he shouted.

Both women ran down the ramp. Tess's heart leaped as she saw Shem leaning back in the front bodyrest. And then she panicked as she realized that she couldn't see Melena anywhere.

"Where's Melena?" she shouted as she came up to Japheth.

Japheth stopped her and hugged her tightly. "Mom, she's . . . our Melena's hurt."

Tess cried out as she ran to the back of the transport and saw Melena lying motionless in the back bodyrest. "What happened?" she asked, sickened by the sight. "What did they do to her?"

"Oh, God, help us," Nusheela said as she came alongside Tess.

"There was . . ." Japheth began. "Mom, I couldn't believe it. She was perfect. She made them think she was totally out of control. They dragged her away, and I had time to get Shem out of that place." He leaned against the transport. "But they beat her, Mom. Over and over again, they beat her. I don't know how she even made it out of there."

While Tess and Nusheela worked together to get Melena out of the transport, Japheth opened the door and pulled Shem out. "I don't think I can make it up that ramp, brother," Shem said weakly.

"You won't have to," Japheth answered. He lifted Shem over his shoulders and began walking up the ramp. He turned slightly to see the two women carrying Melena behind him.

Japheth carried Shem to the back of the entryway and laid him down. Shem leaned back against the wall and looked back at the door. "Go help them," he said.

Japheth took off the protective bodysuit and went to the door. The women were almost to the top. He ran down to help them, but as he took Melena in his arms, he saw another transport coming over the hill. "Look!" he shouted.

Tess and Nusheela turned. They all knew immediately that it was Noah's transport. The bright red color stood out against the green of the trees on the other side of the pathway. Tess and Nusheela hugged and jumped up and down on the ramp.

They watched the transport as it came down the hill and turned toward the gate. Then they looked up and saw several other transports speeding down the hill.

"Who could that be?" Tess said with concern.

"I don't know," said Japheth, also concerned. "I'm going to put Melena down inside and come back out. You two ought to get inside."

Japheth put Melena a safe distance from Shem, who buried his face in his hands when he saw her battered face. Japheth covered her and returned to the door. "Inside, please," he reminded Tess and Nusheela.

Japheth watched as Noah drove through the gate and up to the edge of the ramp next to Japheth's transport. Japheth ran to the door of the transport just as Noah was getting out.

"We got him," Noah said, exhausted. "We had quite a time."

Japheth saw Sicilee getting out of the back. He felt sick when he saw that her face had been beaten and her clothes had been torn. As she stood up, he ran to her. He got there just as she began to fall. "What did they do to you?" he asked angrily.

When she didn't answer, Noah went to him and whispered in his ear. "She was almost at the end of the time, and the man just went . . . he attacked her, ripped her clothes, and hit her in the face. But our God somehow caused the man to panic and run."

Japheth nodded and began to help her up the ramp. Then he remembered the other transports. "Who are they?" he asked.

"It seems it's against the law to take people from the healing center without permission," Noah said without emotion. "Get her on the box and come down to get Ham."

Noah watched as a total of seven transports came through the gate. They encircled Noah and his transport; men and women got out and came straight to him.

"You're under arrest," the first man, a regional commander, said. "You just can't come in and take someone from a healing center."

Another, even larger, man came up next to the first. "I know you have the stolen isolate on there," he said in a surly voice. "You're under arrest, and we're taking the sick man back with us."

More officials came up, many with weapons, all wanting to arrest Noah and his family. Noah looked at Ham, still in the transport, and prayed desperately for deliverance. He felt hands grabbing him from both sides, pulling him away. He looked over again at Ham, and saw two men and a woman opening the door to pull him out. He closed his eyes and cried out loud to God.

Suddenly, the area filled with light. Noah fell to the ground and looked up to see the men who had grabbed him being struck down. All around the workspace, silent, swift avengers cut through the officials. Less than two minutes after the counterattack had begun, the area was quiet once again.

Noah, trembling, pulled himself to his knees. "Praise God," he said softly, his voice choking with emotion. Then, as he slowly looked around him at the evidence of God's deliverence, he fell face down on the ground. "Praise God!" he said, this time louder, as tears filled his eyes.

Then, still on his knees, he lifted his face and hands toward heaven. Overcome with joy, he began to laugh. Then, shouting at the top of his voice, Noah—his face now shining—exclaimed "Praise You, Father!"

Out of the corner of his eye, he saw Jalel standing nearby, weapons in both hands. "What . . . what happened here?" Jalel asked as he looked around the workspace. Noah could see that he was visibly shaken.

"Who . . . who did . . . all this?" Jalel asked, obviously confused. "And where did they go?"

"Jalel," Noah said gently.

Jalel looked at Noah for the first time and was startled at the appearance of Noah's face. Jalel's arms fell helplessly to his side. "What happened to *you*?" Jalel asked, avoiding Noah's gaze.

Noah stood up, still awed by God's powerful rescue. "Jalel," he said, still laughing, "it was the end. It was the very end. They had us." He paused. "No," he corrected himself, "they *thought* they had us. They *thought* they were between us and God's purpose."

Noah began to laugh uncontrollably. "But they were wrong!" he shouted. "God sent his unseen messengers, who struck them down!"

Jalel dropped one of his weapons and reached to hold his head. Noah could see blood on Jalel's hand, and saw that blood saturated the back and side of Jalel's bodysuit.

"That little . . . the woman you had working for you."

"Dainea?" Noah asked, watching with joy as Nusheela threw herself down at Ham's side.

"Yes. Dainea. That woman—she tricked me into untying her." He felt the back of his head. "She almost killed me. I can't believe how much my head aches."

"I'm glad she didn't kill you," Noah said appreciatively.

"Another thing," Jalel said gruffly. "I found that explosive."

"Praise God!" Noah exclaimed.

"Don't I get some credit?" Jalel asked sharply.

"And you," Noah agreed. "Where did you find it?"

"When I came to, while I was still on the ground, I asked myself 'where would I put that if I were a rotten monster like Mizraim.' It came to me—in the common area on the third deck. He'd want to destroy you when you're all together. I had my men pull up the flooring, and there it was."

"Thank you," Noah said gratefully.

"You'll have some flooring to fix on your . . . journey," Jalel said as he looked at the hill.

"Will you be coming with us?" Noah asked sincerely.

Jalel squinted at the hill and shook his head. "No, Seth-Lamech, I don't think so. I have many reasons. In the first place, I just don't think God would want somebody like me. And you told me once that you didn't think I should get on that ship if my heart hadn't changed; well, I just don't see how I could have any real relationship with God with the way I've lived.

"And after seeing what's happened to your family," Jalel continued as he looked up the ramp, "well, it makes me wonder what your God would expect or demand of me. You're decent people, and yet your family is . . ." He looked down at the ground and then into Noah's eyes. Somehow, Jalel's eyes seemed softer than Noah had ever seen them.

"But last of all," Jalel nodded toward the hill, "your friend Mizraim is coming to stop you. I've got one last job to do. I'm going to deal with him and his woman." He looked at Noah and patted him on the shoulder. "And I'm going to do what I can to help give you the fulfillment of your dream. I don't understand it, but you deserve to get on that ship."

Noah's eyes filled with tears. "Later, Jalel," he said sadly, "later when it comes, remember all I've told you about God. You'll know then that I was right. Cry out to God in the name of the serpent-slayer, and He'll take your spirit into Paradise." He touched Jalel's arm. "I'd like to see you there," he said warmly.

The big man allowed himself to smile. "I may forget many things," he said, "but you and this funny ship—never." Then he turned abruptly and walked away.

As Noah went to help Nusheela carry Ham, he looked up to see Jalel's black transport going out the gate. Noah prayed fervently that God would be with Jalel in the trials that he would be facing so very soon.

CHAPTER 28

N oah stood at the door of the ship. Peering into the fading day, he looked for some sign of the coming wrath.

"A hundred and twenty years," he whispered to himself. All that time, and now the day had come. He had pictured this day in his mind a thousand times—he and his family on the ship, the day fading away into blackness and wrath, all of them rejoicing as they saw the evidence becoming visible right before their eyes.

But nothing like that was happening. The day had been, and still was, beautiful, glorious, perfect. The sky looked no different than it ever had. There had been no sounds ever since the far-off battle between Jalel and Mizraim had ended. Even now, Noah prayed for Jalel and hoped he would come to the ship.

And his family was battered. He turned to his left and looked at them, sitting and standing around the entryway. First he saw Melena, who still looked brutalized even after the care Tess had given her. Next was Shem, sitting in the corner and leaning weakly against the wall. Tess had just finished feeding him and was taking off her protective bodysuit.

Nusheela was standing directly behind Noah, in front of the door into the first level. Noah had closed the door to give the family a sense of closeness as they awaited God's move. Nusheela alternated between looking out at the distant city and to her right at Ham, who was awake but lying on a small mat in the other corner. Japheth was sitting on the first step up to the second level, with Sicilee on the floor right next to him.

Noah thought about Methusaleh and wondered if he were still alive. "Dear God," he prayed quietly, "please help that man to see You this day." He also thought about Elimel, and prayed that God would stir him to come while there was still time.

Suddenly, Noah felt the old fear. *What if I was wrong,* the thought came. He knew the voice was the enemy's, but it still made him feel weak. *What if I'm wrong,* he thought again. *What if it gets to the end of the day, and . . .*

"It's so quiet," he heard Tess saying.

He turned to face her. "It is," he agreed. "Almost too quiet. I never expected a lull. I thought we'd get on, and it would come. I never expected . . . this," he said as he swept his arm in the direction of the sky.

"I know," she said. "Neither did I. But the day isn't over yet."

He smiled at her. "I guess we just get our hearts set on how *we* think it's supposed to happen, and . . ." He saw her smiling at him. "I *am* concerned that if it takes very long, the regional government will send out more men to find out what happened here. And I remember people telling me that they were going to come and block us in."

She came up to his side and whispered in his ear. "We're in God's hands now," she encouraged. "There's nothing more we can do."

And he knew she was right. "Dear God," he prayed into her ear, "I give all my fears to You. I give this project to You. It's all Yours, anyway. I ask that You help me to rest in You and trust that You'll do everything in a perfect way."

As he finished praying he heard Japheth say "Dad, look!" Noah turned and looked at the sky and city, both unchanged. And then he looked down and saw someone standing at the bottom of the ramp. A man was looking over the ship, while he smiled and nodded in approval.

Excitement filled Noah as he watched the man begin to walk slowly up the ramp. The man walked straight toward Noah and stopped just a few cubits away — close enough to touch him.

The man's face was soft and very familiar. Noah could feel the tension leaving his body in the presence of this friend.

The man walked past Noah and Tess to Melena. He bent down to the ground and took her face in his hands. He whispered something to her, and then he kissed her. When he stood up and helped her to her feet, Noah could see that her face had been completely restored.

As the man walked the short distance to Shem, Noah knew in his heart what this man was going to do. Noah watched as Shem stood to greet the visitor, and rejoiced as he saw the man touch Shem. He watched Shem move his arms around freely, the weakness all gone. "Praise God!" he heard Shem say. Shem suddenly jumped into the air. "Praise God!" he shouted. Melena ran to him, and they hugged each other tightly.

Noah saw that Nusheela was trembling as the man walked to her. Noah watched him whisper in her ear and saw her nodding in agreement. She looked over at Sicilee and formed her mouth into the words "please forgive me." Sicilee understood and nodded her agreement.

The man walked toward Ham, who was crying and moaning. As the man bent down and touched Ham's face, Noah could hear Ham saying, "I'm sorry—forgive me." He saw the man nod and then stand. The man looked lovingly down at Ham, until Ham finally understood and got to his feet. Ham's face was beaming as he looked around at the others and rejoiced in his healing.

Then Ham dropped to his knees and took the man's hand, holding it to his face and then kissing it. Noah pulled Tess close, and they rejoiced together in what they were seeing. Nusheela, crying with overflowing joy, went to Ham, knelt down next to him, and buried her face in his chest.

The man then walked to Sicilee, whose eyes were shining in anticipation. He put his hands on her face, and the wounds and bruises disappeared. He leaned forward and whispered in her ear. She smiled and nodded, and with quiet boldness kissed him on the cheek.

Then he went to Japheth. The others drew closer to see what would happen. "I want to see," Japheth said quietly. The man nodded and hugged him. The man touched his own mouth, and then put his fingers on the blind eye. "I can see!" Japheth exclaimed in a loud whisper. "Dear God, I can see!"

As the man walked toward Noah and Tess, the others formed a small circle around them. The man stopped in front of them and looked intently into their faces. He leaned forward and whispered for a long time into Tess's ear. Then he took Noah's hand and led him a few steps to the edge of the ramp.

And suddenly, Noah knew who the man was. He knew, in a way he couldn't explain, that his great ancestor, Adam, had looked into those same eyes, sensed that same power, felt that same deep compassion and love. He knew that this man was no man at all, that somehow he was face-to-face with the living God.

Then this man — this God — reached out His hand and touched Noah's tired face. The touch turned into a gentle caress, the shining face broke into an appreciative smile. Noah felt a surge of emotion that choked him and brought tears to his eyes.

He knew then that what he had done for many years by faith had now been blessed by the unforgettable and wonderful sight of the Man who had shared cool evening walks with Adam so many years before.

And then the God-man nodded, and Noah knew that the time had come. Noah stepped back, just inside the door. The Man turned and walked down the ramp a few steps.

Noah watched as the Man looked at the city, glistening in the twilight. And then he saw tears flowing down the Man's cheeks, and Noah realized that this God-man, even in His holiness and justice, was grieving with a heart full of pain over this lost and rebellious people, people He had made with His very own hands.

And then Noah remembered. He saw in his mind the old painting that he had seen in the lavish God-house so long ago. Almost without thinking, he looked down at the feet of this awesome Man. There, even in the deepening shadows, Noah could see the heel of a foot that had been bitten by a snake.

As the God-man turned to face him again, Noah looked just past Him at the twilight now descending on the magnificent city of his birth. His eyes surveyed the towers stretching from one end of the horizon to the other, haunting in the darkening mist. And then he looked once more at his visitor smiling back at him, and he knew he had made the right choice.

He saw the arm go up to reach for the door, and he rejoiced as he realized that the one, true God was sealing him in, as he had tucked his own children into bed so many years before. The scene before him narrowed, and the far-off sounds faded, as the door slammed shut.

And in the distance Noah heard a mighty roar.

ABOUT THE AUTHOR

J ames R. Lucas shepherds the Living Faith Church in Shawnee Mission, Kansas. He is the author of the Christian novel, *Weeping in Ramah* (Crossway Books), and the non-fiction challenge to parents, *The Parenting of Champions: Raising Godly Children in an Evil Age* (Wolgemuth & Hyatt, Publishers, Inc.).

Mr. Lucas has been a management executive with several different companies, and the president of Luman Consultants, a management consulting firm. He lives with his wife, Pam, and their four children, Laura, Peter, David, and Bethany, in Prairie Village, Kansas.

The typeface for the text of this book is *Times Roman*. In 1930, typographer Stanley Morison joined the staff of *The Times* (London) to supervise design of a typeface for the reformatting of this renowned English daily. Morison had overseen type-library reforms at Cambridge University Press in 1925, but this new task would prove a formidable challenge despite a decade of experience in paleography, calligraphy, and typography. *Times New Roman* was credited as coming from Morison's original pencil renderings in the first years of the 1930s, but the typeface went through numerous changes under the scrutiny of a critical committee of dissatisfied *Times* staffers and editors. The resulting typeface, *Times Roman*, has been called the most used, most successful typeface of this century. The design is of enduring value to English and American printers and publishers, who choose the typeface for its readability and economy when run on today's high-speed presses.

Substantive Editing:
Michael S. Hyatt

Copy Editing:
Susan Kirby

Cover Design:
Steve Diggs & Friends
Nashville, Tennessee

Page Composition:
Xerox Ventura Publisher
Printware 720 IQ Laser Printer

Printing and Binding:
Maple-Vail Book Manufacturing Group
York, Pennsylvania

Cover Printing:
Strine Printing Company
York, Pennsylvania

Christian Jr./Sr High School
2100 Greenfield Dr
El Cajon, CA 92019